P9-DWG-131

INNOCENCE

a novel

LOUIS B. JONES

COUNTERPOINT
BERKELEY

Library of Congress Cataloging-in-Publication Data
Jones, Louis B.
 Innocence / Louis B. Jones.
   pages cm
  ISBN 978-1-61902-066-5 (pbk.)
  I. Title.
  PS3560.O516I56 2013
  813'.54—dc23   2012040588

Cover design by Debbie Berne
Interior design by Erin Seaward-Hiatt

COUNTERPOINT
1919 Fifth Street
Berkeley, CA 94710
www.counterpointpress.com

Printed in the United States of America
Distributed by Publishers Group West

10 9 8 7 6 5 4 3 2 1

INNOCENCE

DR. AUCTOR ALWAYS looked like a plausible surgeon, if only because he was so handsome. Which, alone, isn't a cause for trust but is oddly relevant in a cosmetic surgeon, artificer of beauty. In Dr. Auctor, the delicacy of eyebrow and the calm sharpness of eye, the clear forehead, the crest of shiny black sculpted hair, symmetry of jaw and temple—and most of all, his tininess, because he stood only about chest-high—in his especial miniaturization he seemed to glint with a supernatural sharpness of focus. When I first met him, in the corridor of his clinic, the elfin handshake grip seemed exactly right. Inarguably, my lip is a success. He must know what he's doing. The mask of perfect normalcy cupping my face is something I wonder if I'll ever get used to. My palate, too—strange new surface in my mouth, cemented by live flesh and bone—resounds with usefulness. My tongue taps it in speaking. My oatmeal in the morning meets it, and is defeated. It was amazing how I got accustomed right away to having the low ceiling inside my mouth as a working surface. Healing has gone fast, just as he promised. As a professional his advice was always brisk, his decisions always quick and calm. He obviously learned his craft somewhere. Even if it were true that his first awkward scalpel strokes, conceivably, were attempted outside the walls of a medical school, still my own lip and the fine post-op features of everyone in our Recovery Group are evidence that he's an artist. His longtime patients testify that their tissues have aged well, long after their surgery.

Therefore, when an email rumor traveled around the Recovery Group that our Dr. Auctor had been accused (twenty-five years ago, in another state) of practicing medicine without a proper education, I personally as a satisfied patient was unable to doubt him: I pictured him surrounded by his hospital affiliations, his expensive equipment, all his support personnel, his clinic at a good address. Most convincing of all, I had my very useful new face, which hadn't lifted to a permanent snarl, or flaked off onto my pillow, or, fairy tale–wise, sprouted a horn overnight, comeuppance for vanity. The rumor held that Dr. Auctor was practicing as what the AMA calls a "cookbook surgeon," that is, home-taught, uneducated, home-rehearsed.

Some few days after the subsequent gossipy, scandalized Recovery Group meeting (this all happened on the weekend of the big tristate power failure), I was home at my rectory desk on Saturday morning—I had an appointment later in the afternoon to drive over to the little neighborhood of Gerstle Park for an inspection on a 3br/1ba listing I have in escrow there—when my desk phone rang. It was a certain woman from Group, by the name of Thalia, with news that would exonerate Dr. Auctor. Records of old legal proceedings showed he'd been acquitted of all such suspicions.

I was already complacent about the whole matter: Auctor is plainly, effectively, the real thing. Rather, the more alarming, unhoped-for new development was that this woman—her name is Thalia, as I've said—was calling with the ulterior purpose of inviting me on a weekend in the country. Just the two of us. Starting right then. Immediately. I was to drop everything. It took her a while to get around to saying it. One night at a fancy lodge. She'd already gone ahead and made reservations, no doubt as scared as I. There are certain anatomical matters between us we haven't faced, complications peculiar to the genetic condition

we happen to share, which would never come up for polite discussion in Group. She and I haven't had any way of mentioning
our anatomies. And undiscussed matters will have a way of sinking to total undiscussability, there to swell and bloat in silence.
Meanwhile, the biological clock does tick. It ticks for men as for
women, perhaps at a different rate but just as irreversibly. Marriage is actually named as a "vocation" in the old Catholic catechism—that is, a "calling," like the priesthood. I could certainly
never have been a Catholic, but I'm a remote admirer of their
radicalism: the vocation to marriage is supposedly "written by
the hand of the Creator into the very nature of man and woman."
Imagine those charitable old frizzy celibates in the Vatican, pens
in hand, thinking how men's and women's anatomies happen to
puzzle together. Thalia and I have kissed. That has happened. It
happened last week. We were standing at the time, embracing
in her doorway, and while it was happening we were both aware
of inevitable nether collisions, wherein the marriage vocation is
written into our natures. She's in her twenties.

She's in her *late* twenties, more accurately, and I admit during
these weeks, since I joined Recovery Group—since the moment
I first saw her—she has been on my mind frequently in ways I
don't feel entitled to. She may be a post-op "bunny," but she is
authoritative in beauty, and obviously always has been so, all her
life, despite any erstwhile labial flaw. She's a woman who, at all
times, shows a bright expectation of others' gazes, even sidewise
upon her nape, or her cheek, her omniscient cheek. Such open
celebrity can, for the shyer, act as an exclusion; I personally rather
veer from any limelight, whereas she walks in limelight. As a
child, she underwent cosmetic restorations that were competent,
if not perfect; her generation in that decade was one of the first
to benefit from a certain then-experimental, awful device that
squashes an infant's lip flesh to train it to grow together. (We
all bring our pre-op photos in to Group.) Having now a perfect
new lip, as she does, will encourage a self-confidence, but this is
more; this is a force of beauty inborn in her body. In the Recovery

Group circle, on her metal folding chair, she tends to sit with a gymnastic restless bounce of the hip.

Given what's at stake between us, when she made the abrupt proposal of a weekend in the country, she was taking over authority in both of our lives as the architect of our fate, and in that instant, in submission I was passing through a doorway of *her* design. Nothing is light or inconsequential, nothing meaningless. Everything is weighted from the start. Everything "doomed," you might say. The end is built into the beginning. And here's a home truth, which I could always resort to, if I were to see events adding up to disaster: a soul equipped for *solitude* is a well-equipped soul.

I know all this, perfectly well. Yet the phone rings and the entire castle of solitude evaporates; one forgets wisdom instantly and dog-paddles straight out, joyfully out, into foolishness. Says Ecclesiastes: it's better to go to the house of mourning than the house of feasting. And elsewhere: the fool's heart is in the house of mirth. All this isn't just "the Bible"; it's the facts. It's life. When I picked up the phone, the pretty female voice asking for "John Gegenuber" with no trace of hypernasal resonance was the voice of my still-unbelievable Thalia, the same woman I had kissed the week before on her doorstep. For her to pick up her phone and freely call me was a confirmation that the kiss wasn't a dream or fantasy or regrettable mistake; such a phone call was an endorsement of the kiss, a ratification of a kiss's contractual quality a week later, on a sunny Saturday. And I was able to reply, "Speaking," though not long ago I'd have said "smeaking"—(or *"thmeengking,"* Lord!)—despite years of speech therapy. All my life the surname Gegenuber, laden with plosive consonants, has been an unlucky one, and I have always pronounced it with a mocked smile, smile of apology, smile of irony and hopelessness, *Zhon Ngay-ngen-ummer,* the ugly glottal stops and hypernasal resonances all in a buzzing swarm in my midst. Developmentally it's in grade school, it's around second grade, that this thing "shame" sets in. When Thalia phoned I was able to speak as a

handsome impostor. Her call happened to come when I was surf-
ing through Internet pornography clips in my rectory (as I continue to call it). And for a panicky second while her voice in the
receiver entered into friendly gossip, onscreen a woman kept on
going, pretending to be abjectly insatiable, my hand hunting for
the QUIT button, eyes too scalded blind to locate it, my entire soul
suddenly a mere lingering wisp of sulfur in the room. Poking into
these sites is a meaningless safari for a forty-nine-year-old, which
originally I pardoned because it's a fitting part of middle age and
futurelessness. Back in my adolescence, any possible visits to the
popular *schmutzig* magazines of the day, on the newsstands, were
a matter of hopefulness, research, preparing for real possibili-
ties, while I scanned the airbrushed centerfold model displayed
and garnished like the prizewinning pig at the county fair; these
days the style is more explicit and naturalistic. Now that I'm near
fifty, it's been not hope but rather hopelessness—hopelessness's
peculiar solace—that licensed these occasional moments of indo-
lent desire and envy. It was long before I laid eyes on Thalia that
I discovered the new virtual, cramped world. Now I have met
her; and we have together shown our willingness to, perhaps,
pass through that "doorway" of her design, yet I come again in
moments of boredom to make reconnaissance of such stupid
websites, because, I suppose, it's taken on an aspect of hope and
study again. It all first thrusts itself at you in the form of advertisements, and I think I went on exploring its glossy, miniature,
Dantesque world because of the sheer astonishment—you might
say admiration—for how highly developed and far-reaching is
the kingdom of sin and delight.

Envy is called one of the seven capital sins. In the practice
of this particular inconsequential vice, "envy" holds hands with
"lust," another of the seven. Usually "gluttony," too, puts in an
appearance on these mornings, when that *capital*-capital sin
boredom—the unofficial eighth, and the mysterious gateway to
the other seven—leadeth me beside the still waters. *Accidie* is the
theologian's more comprehensive word to describe this spiritual

condition. This particular Saturday was typical: I had hours to kill before an appointment at a Gerstle Park corner-lot bungalow with a home inspector and the buyers' agent. On this morning my gluttony had taken the form of a second bowl of Raisin Bran with skim milk, which was more than I wanted; surely I was trying with its soggy mass to dampen the headache of last night's (also gluttonous) indulgence in that one last extra, excessive, superfluous, redundant glass of wine. The old popish church in her wisdom called certain sins "capital" because they serve as "the head," i.e., the thinking part, for other "subsequent and consequent errors." (I will always love the old legalistic poetry. I might have gone Catholic if I'd had the stomach for all the weirdly lit drama. It's an absolute religion, a thoroughgoingly intellectual religion, a religion only for the most inwardly scrupulous. Those people really *intend* to end as saints.) Supposedly it's the "subsequent and consequent errors" that are the mortal sins—i.e., sins more specific, more grievous, more ruinous in their results than a little bit of lust and gluttony. People in this enlightened age may chuckle, but "sin" continues to furnish a nice tool of psychology. Even in Marin County of the twenty-first century, during my years in a Sausalito parish, the old medieval razor-sharp distinction *sin* kept coming out of its little black velvet carrying case, a practical tool of psychoanalysis more useful than the Freudian cartoon the "id." Or that other mythological thing, "the collective unconscious." Unlike those new evasions, sin is right at hand, like a fork, or like a steering wheel, or a computer mouse or a TV remote. It's right there. Sin. You're in it. You point and click with it.

For an Episcopal minister in Marin County, sin has provided a vast playground of work. And in my own personal psychology, the lust/gluttony/envy trio has led to nothing terrible in the way of the subsequent and consequent sins. I'm hedged about with considerations, always. An early-in-life devotion in seminary builds a dam in a man's heart, which will probably always be a solid indestructible thing. (Almost as solid a dam as a congenital harelip.) And, too, when it comes to judging myself, I'm lenient. For when it comes to judgment, one *is* one's "fellow man" in eternity, *oneself*, with whom one is condemned to spend one's everlasting reward. And one goes easy. In my newer profession in Marin real estate, I have found certain other sins to be more treacherous than the lust/gluttony combo. Wrath for example is a sweet one, its raptures and transports a kick to an ambitious man; and avarice, of course, in real estate, it's a kind of fuel or food we all run on, at a cellular-metabolism level; pride, too, the chief of the seven—all are necessities in business, all to be judged as leniently in my fellow realtor as I might hope they can be judged in myself. According to scripture, such kinder sins—as the concupiscence here on my computer screen—are made of mere "wood, hay, and stubble": they will be gathered up and burned in the cleansing fire at last gratefully. That was the charitable view of the Pauline Epistles, and it survived over the centuries to take the same form in Aquinas. Here on my computer screen is the Earth's wood, hay, and stubble, in the very form of woman's ecstasy; and in my blessed irrelevance on my own side of the screen (the oddly dimmer and unreal side of the screen, sometimes it seems), I see a man's and woman's play *not* as a divagation from God's will (Augustinian definition of sin) but, of course, a fulfillment of God's will. At the moment when my desk phone rang, this particular cheerleader (or housewife or nympho or piano teacher or whatever; there's always some minor dramatic conceit; and for the actors a cliché dash of characterization) had been lifted and churned to such mindless gratitude and audacity I weirdly felt I couldn't desert the poor actress, as witness of her extremity. In the video clip it seemed pretty clear—(and this fact crucially helps; maybe it somewhat exculpates an old sinner; it's a *sine qua non*, in fact)—it at least seemed evident that the actress was an intelligent, alert human being. Realistically I suppose, in that industry, most of the actresses are patently not smart, or are even dulled by the drugs that may keep them in that lifestyle. But in the case of this woman I was sure I recognized the flicker of wisdom. It's the sort of woman I've always thought I would never have the good luck to know. At least during this, my own brief "slot of light." She would have to be a chimera.

I did, of course, stop the video; in panic and shame I hit the QUIT button and banished those silly devils, because the holier voice of Thalia, all unknowing, in her separate sphere, spoke in my ear. She began, "I thought I'd call, because guess what."

She would take the role of the talkative one. I was not entitled, ethically, to use my own voice freely, not for a minute or two, an impostor indeed.

She said she'd had a phone call about Dr. Auctor from one of our friends in Group—a certain Margot. Margot is a woman I'd have considered a much likelier candidate than Thalia, for my friendship, because Margot has a philosophy A.B.D. (All-But-Dissertation) from Brown and is sarcastic and discontented, funny, cynical, repellent, needy. More my type.

Anyway our friend Margot, according to Thalia, had gotten in touch with a medical review board in New York State. She had requested copies of the old transcripts of Dr. Auctor's long-ago trial. And the transcripts indicated that he had shown, way back then, documentary proof of his medical education and residency. He had gotten his medical degree at an overseas school; however, it was a real school. It was an accredited school. Also, according to Margot, he didn't appear on quackwatch.com, while he *did* appear on a website of California board-certified surgeons.

Our friend Margot—and this is an excellent development in *her* emotional situation—had clearly started to enjoy her role as snoop. She is an interesting, worrisome case; and Thalia and I, for a while then, got on to the topic of Margot herself. She has been a subject of general concern lately among the Recovery Groupers because she attempted suicide this spring. She swallowed her entire supply of antidepressant pills, washing them down with a carbonated energy drink called Rockstar. Having done so, she sat down to watch the Weather Channel—and then quickly, wisely, got scared and called an ambulance.

(The Weather Channel is a nice detail. Personally, I like to picture Margot's crisis of repentance coming at the moment when she started caring about the next day's weather.)

Facial reconstruction—the acquisition of a whole new "person" to speak through the mouth-hole of—is a traumatic psychic event. It's especially traumatic for those who've lived their entire lives with an important disfigurement. Readjusting can have emotional pitfalls. A kind of confusion can go on for months or recur over years. In the case of Margot, her operation was a minor one. She isn't like us harelips and bifurcated mandibles and hemangiomas and laceration-mutilation cases. All she'd had was a nose job, repairing an odd bulbousness. But like all of us, she believed she was entering into a more beautiful new form—and did enter into a more beautiful new form!—but there is a mysterious tricky false bottom to the treasure chest of human nature: a certain consummate despair can come with the satisfaction of longing. Among post-ops, people with new faces can, as the phrase in Group has it, come "unstuck from their lives." We human beings are profound: we are profound and yet we are devoted to a conscious shallowness. In my years as a minister with a parish in Sausalito, I was continually surprised. It's bizarre, how people's construction of themselves and their purpose in the world can be flimsy, amazingly flimsy, and they want to keep it that way. When I had a parish, this general, popular preference for self-ignorance grew, over the years, into the monster I was born to do battle with. Most people's lives are devised to be, merely, a constant hectic distraction. It's likely that Margot's particular weakness, whatever it was, has been complicated by a divorce, which took place during the year before her plastic surgery. If I had to guess, I'd say "wrath" is one of Margot's dark pleasures. In her case I've wondered if cosmetic surgery was supposed to be a kind of vengeance. Against the happy irresponsible ex-husband. Whom we used to hear a bit too much about, in Group.

Anyway, she was doing well now. This week Thalia had taken her out shopping, so she said. They went into San Francisco, downtown, and they bought shoes. They bought interesting kitchen equipment. (She was going on, telling me all this, while I tilted back in the creaky leather desk chair that originated in my old, actual rectory. I happen to love that creak. I happen to be a great listener.) They had a drink at Fog City. They went to the farmers' market at the Ferry Building. They bought some kind of wonderful rubber gadget that removes garlic cloves' tough husks. They bought exotic and delicious things, good olive oil from a Marin ranch, incredibly expensive wild morels. Dirt clung to the morels, which added to their weight on the grocer's scale.

And then, in a warp-speed non sequitur (reminding me how much younger she is than I, and how brave I will have to be), she concluded, "So, John, let's meet today! Let's have a rendezvous and be investigators. And look further into the mysterious case of Dr. Auctor before it all blows away. Let's meet in a seamy little bar, cloak-and-dagger-style. I've got a plan. Let's wear disguises."

"Today? Now?"

I had my appointment in Gerstle Park, but I could cancel it. In my mind, I could summon Thalia's eyes, their sparkle and evasion. And the lovely tendons in her neck, and in her shoulder. Once, on a warm day in Group, she arrived in a sleeveless shirt. In the circle, I always sit a little behind and to the left of her. That was a great day.

"Here's my plan. It's very Nancy Drew. I have to take the Green Thumbs landscaping crew up to Sonoma tomorrow."

Thalia makes her living as a so-called horticultural therapist. Horticultural therapy is what she took her college degree in, and Green Thumbs is the organization she works for. They employ developmentally disabled adults as landscape gardeners.

"I think I mentioned in Group," she went on, "that Green Thumbs has *his* landscaping account. If you come with me, we can go up there. Today. To his place."

I said, "Dr. Auctor's account?"

She had, in fact, mentioned it in Group, but I was absent from the circle that week and learned such things by hearsay; to be honest, I learned this by aggressively debriefing some of the other Groupers on the topic of Thalia. Still, I acted as if this were news to me because I didn't want to seem to have been inquiring about her.

"But he's not there now. He's in Europe. His place will be empty. We could go there, John. With my landscaping-crew guys. And at least have a nice picnic lunch, while the gang works."

All this dodging and feinting, I suddenly liked to think, was a test of my tolerance for caprice, so crucial in a husband. In fact, she was trying to summon up the courage to ask me on an over-night trip to a spa, but none of that had emerged yet. I was still trying to picture the seamy little bar she'd mentioned.

"Wouldn't you like to work outdoors today? Just for fun? And get inside the gates of Dr. Auctor's home place? With my merry men?"

"I'm supposed to be at an inspection on a house in Gerstle Park," I pleaded, but my tone of voice was all happy connivance, all submission, because in my heart I had forgotten all wisdom. I knew again what it felt like being a teenager, being on the phone with a female in all her instant authority, in particular with a female who, I would think, should have better men to pursue than me, and who seemed to be proposing wonderful mischief, of some kind—because this chase was going to lead elsewhere—and I was completely willing to give up all my plans and throw myself into a rendezvous in a "seamy little bar" and afterward appar-ently lurk in Dr. Auctor's shrubbery with pruners and shears—it was all too preposterous to be anything but enchantment. The bar that appeared in my mind, the only describable "seamy little bar" I'd ever noticed in all of Marin, was an old place on Fourth Street that was still holding its ground, Bunce's, a sticky, dark, recessed trap. Inside, in one of those banquette booths, those cof-fin-upholstered shells in red vinyl (as I pictured the place), Thalia would be wearing a luminous ivory sweater, a sweater she'd worn on two occasions in Recovery Group. Which, in a sticky joint like Bunce's, would have a fitting, defiant radiance. My adolescent obsession with the female form is so deep-planted, the sudden knob between my eyes that hardens to a spike so dims my vision, the radiance of a sweater is a glory to forbid the eye, and also repel the hand. She would order white wine in a stemmed glass. Yes, and so would I. Wine in the middle of the day. Her fingernail would lightly, idly, stroke and pluck the vertical strand of glass supporting the goblet. And she would lay out her piratical plan for visiting Dr. Auctor's property in the guise of landscape gardeners, along with her crew of retarded adults. Or rather, no, if that was how things were to unfold, she wouldn't wear the ivory sweater; she'd be dressed for outdoor work. I would have to dress roughly, too.

"I need to at least *contact* the buyers' agent," I said, revolving my desk chair away from the computer screen, to banish, all the more, the brimstone in my study, facing my bookshelves instead. That I had ever been an Episcopal minister, Thalia had no idea. It's a revelation I get around to when I know people better. "I've got an older lady in Gerstle Park who is selling. I really ought not to cancel the meeting."

Thalia and I both knew I was going to cancel the meeting. And reschedule.

And so betray my client. It pained me to think of disappointing Mrs. Goodkind, ninety-one-year-old Edna Goodkind, her eyes packed deep in remote heavenly dusts and distances. A sweet heroine still, a vestal to the memory of her husband, she resisted the cleaning and simplifying of her 3br/1ba when it needed to be staged for open houses. It had to be cleared of all its grime and most of its furniture, stripped of all the (objectively unpleasant) artifacts on the walls from the Goodkinds' voyages, and the neatly catalogued ichthyology magazines, all in order on the shelves, which she goes on renewing subscriptions to, even though her husband the ichthyologist has been dead for years. She says she might donate them to "a major institution somewhere," and then she could (this is how Edna imagines the world works) take a big tax write-off on the fantastic value of the whole library, because a couple of the old issues contained articles on extinct fish written forty years ago by her husband. Packaging up Mrs. Goodkind for the handoff to an assisted-living facility makes me a dark angel enough. Worse is to deprive her of her old ichthyology journals. Which will land in the Dumpster, surely.

A reader may not believe this: the spiritual fulfillments in being a real estate agent are equal to—higher than!—the spiritual fulfillments of having a thriving parish. Church, too, is showbiz—church is social and corrupt and turbulent like real estate—and I find I use the same skill set; a clergyman's life is an enterprising or even entrepreneurial life, a life of charisma and people skills and rhetoric, and a few clever moves with a budget—especially these days, with competition from all the big new churches, not just the kinds they call "mega" but the "middle-mega-churches" popping up out there, the people-pleasin', one-size-fits-all nondenominationals that are springing up in satellite zones of regional malls. (Indeed from a commercial real estate standpoint they occupy the very same traffic-pattern locations as malls do, and *might have been* Walmarts or Home Depots rather than the Lord's house.) Still, in my new life, a pastor's façade continues to stick to me. It clings although the added sticky spot of the harelip is no longer there. This morning, even as I foresaw myself sitting at a gummy old banquette table, in Bunce's with Thalia, there, too, I could only envision myself wearing the face of a priest; everyone knows the priest face, sheer yet accessible. It's the way I always took power. By pastorality. And by deformity. For here is another unlikely fact about deformity: a freak, like an impossibly beautiful woman in the room, can pretty much get what he wants, and wields some power.

Thalia then said, "Oh! In fact! I want to buy a house. Let's do that today, too, if we can fit it in. Let's buy a house."

I had long ago started to get the point; she was, *herself,* the hunt. And I'd been swept into her world, and I had already forsaken Mrs.

Goodkind. So shameless and happy is man. My screen saver hadn't yet kicked in, and the screen was blank but for my few usual stale icons, <house-listing.pdf> emblems, client profiles, investments and charities, downloaded Internet articles, credit reports. I said, turning away from all that, "Well, are you serious? You know, business is kinda slow. I could use a client. What kind of house are you looking for?" I put my shod feet up, like a rude self-assured stranger, upon the opposite bookshelf, where stand the spines of Tillich and Rahner, Nietzsche and Kierkegaard and Freud and Jung, Tanakh and Veda, concordance and encyclopedia, which once provided, and I guess still do, the rooms of my labyrinth.

WHAT DID I know about Thalia so far?

There were important things I didn't know. One thing I hadn't yet heard was her last name. In Group, surnames aren't used, and between us it hadn't come up, though we'd gone out twice, and even kissed. The scarier unexplored topic, "the dark side of the moon" to us, was the possibility of certain other deformities that I've alluded to. It will be common knowledge among us "bunnies" who are the slightest bit well-informed, palatal bifurcation often goes along with other abnormalities along the body's ventral meridian, frenum, philtrum, et cetera. Something about the lay of Thalia's various silences around those topics (a golf fairway's out-of-the-way sand traps and water hazards) made me feel that she might have other surgical secrets. Or that she might guess of mine. During that minute in her doorway when we did kiss, along with an intoxication arose a dread or just reluctance, palpable in her spine, a thread there whose tautness was more serious than mere fear. More practical.

Things I did know. I knew she had a degree in psychology, in a discipline called horticultural therapy, working with mentally or emotionally handicapped people in gardens. I knew she was employed by this place Green Thumbs. I knew she lived in a freeway-side neighborhood of Novato, because I'd dropped her off at home, beside the rumble and swish of 101, and that she considered herself lucky and prosperous, to be living there, because it was a "pool complex" and included "a club membership," with "a clubhouse." As a minister I've seen couples' class-background inequalities furnish a positive delight, in marriages' early years. It's only later in a marriage, when choices depend on values, that differences in sophistication can cause trouble. I'm not talking about snobbery as a force in a marriage but something, frankly, perilously close to it. In sharing life choices, people can overcome their differences in education and experience and class. It's one of the ways they grow as human beings. As a sometime spiritual counselor, in these class-nervous California suburbs, I've sometimes seen a human being grow by shrinking, paradoxically.

Another thing about Thalia—this was something neither of us could ignore: she was twenty years younger. But an age difference really didn't seem material. Developmentally, there seems to be a point in the third decade of life when boys at last catch up with girls, after which point one or the other gender's relative "maturity" is an open controversy. She's a lot quicker and cleverer than I, all my pretensions notwithstanding. In choosing me, she would be choosing, perhaps, to be one of those women who are granted two lives, one as a wife, then a second as a widow. It's a pair of consecutive lives many women lead with a lot of satisfaction, and I've seen widowhood sometimes be as fulfilling as even a great first marriage, with a little luck and fortuitous timing.

I won't apologize for letting my imagination range forward into the future. One does, in life, try to take some control of what's inevitable. One does compose various alternative versions of a future. This is how I am. By the time I was getting into my car that morning to go meet her, I was thinking about prenuptial agreements. I do have a bit of wealth, a small, very ordinary bit, sitting and wasting, while it naturally grows by itself. It's something I'd be bringing to the marriage. Thalia comes from hardworking people in Montana and got through four years at the state college there afloat on the long pontoon bridge of scholarships and student loans. And her mother is still alive, living in a government-subsidized home, presumably a necessitous old lady. My lawyer will insist on a prenuptial agreement that puts my assets into a trust, but I plan on contravening him, because not only is this a matter of principle with me, but also I would feel absolutely relieved to turn over my small treasure to Thalia unconditionally. I have no children to provide for, nor needy nephews getting an education. My lawyer—an unbending, unlaughing man with the improbable name (really a litigious name!) of Victor Person—will be adamant about my never giving up my rights beforehand, because that's his job, as my attorney, to have absolutely no sense of humor, so that I may keep mine. But Victor will have to be overruled. According to my own philosophy it's important to ensure that our separate small pots of money are combined, mine and Thalia's, if our "troth" ever be "plighted." Over the years as a minister—and moreover as a realtor!—I have learned and relearned how right it is that a couple's shiny gold should be comingled, with no expectation of "justice" in this world. Even in materialistic Marin, it's been my experience that people can be guided by the force of a greater love even when they don't think they are, or don't want to be. Thalia and I, anyway, will have paper bank checks printed that announce both husband and wife jointly. Unless of course she happens to have other ideas. All to be aired in a prenup.

In any case, I got in my car wearing jeans and a T-shirt and a flannel shirt. I looked as if I were ready to prune roses, or hoe dirt.

But the dirt-hoeing duds felt now like merely a costume and a ruse. The plan for the weekend had changed, dramatically, during our phone conversation, and I was also bringing my overnight suitcase, including even a bathing suit. We would probably do some digging in gardens, on the following day, but today and tonight would be something unimaginable. And there would be no drink at Bunce's either. That idea had been discarded, which was a relief; I've always found drinking wine at noontime wrecks an afternoon, somehow *insults* an afternoon.

Instead, what emerged was her real plan. At a point when I was admitting I might try to excuse myself somehow from the meeting at Edna Goodkind's house, Thalia interrupted me by blurting out, "John, I want to do the Napa winery tour."

Since I wasn't sure whether this desire was to involve me, I couldn't respond right away, and she went on, "You know, sipping, sniffing, spitting in the little pot, standing around, like in colonnades. It's going to be a beautiful weekend. The fact is, I reserved a room at a spa for tonight. I can arrange to forget about my Green Thumbers. Let Sandy take them out today. And we can do the picnic-basket thing, the roadster-parked-in-the-meadow, the wearing tam-o'-shanters, the whole thing. Do you golf? I've never golfed! In my life! Never! Never in my life!"

"Do you mean overnight?" I said, and then quick, "I do happen to know a few of the wineries. I'd be an excellent guide."

"Wine I'm a dork about. But I'm willing to try learning."

She's so alienly physically pretty in the face, her voice so meltingly intelligent, I had this odd sci-fi vision of the two of us on the phone connection, differently gendered bipeds making intelligible noises to each other, with new faces like scuba gear, on our separate telephones negotiating this tryst. Flippers, air-supply tubes, weight belts, the whole outfit, while hatching a romantic rendezvous.

"The back roads," I was saying, "That's what you want. In Napa, there are two roads. The main highway and the other one. What you want is the other one. And the littler ones."

"I'm not going to say my taste is discriminating."

"Presumably, I could . . . pack a suitcase, and then—?"

"Oh! Oh! I'll have to call Sandy and arrange this. I'm sure she'll be fine with it."

"Going north-south, there's the little ladder of back-and-forth roads. Most people tend to stay on the highway and only visit the big commercial wineries."

"Probably cold chicken?" she said. "Cold asparagus? Things like that?"

Then there was a lull.

"Where?" I said, not meaning to sound so grim.

"The Silverado," she said. It was a place pictured in magazine advertisements, in champagne-colored light with masseuses and fluffy towels. A one-night reservation would have cost her some part of a week's salary. It also has hot tubs; they make eclipsed appearances in the ads, in the backgrounds, where fumes rise. Soon we managed to hang up, calling out to each other through the scuba masks, "Excellent." "Great." "I'm looking forward to it." "All right, then." "Great."

So in my driveway, I had put my little suitcase in the trunk, and I pricked the engine into action and moved the gearshift to put it in gear, but then, foot on the brake, I paused for one little visit to the realistic present moment to look at my image in the rearview mirror, the small jiggling envelope-shaped world there, fixed to assert itself above the windshield's broader revelation of the future. What I saw, reflected back at me—as I revolved my jawline, and my hairline—was a regular-featured man of forty-nine with a full head of green-blonde hair (because I swim in a chlorinated pool) and two rows of well-lined-up blazing-white teeth, a man handsome enough to be unprincipled.

Handsome enough to be capable of betraying Edna Good-kind, I was setting out on a romantic adventure, leaving Mrs. Goodkind to confront, alone, those dimwit reptiles Shawn and Cheese, the couple who were buying her house. Shawn and Cheese—he with his rock guitarist's pallor, she with her rock groupie's tedious just-been-raped look—are the callow, rich, sub-urban children, unmarried, who have made the winning offer on Mrs. Goodkind's bungalow. They're the only offer, actually. Busi-ness is presently slow and sticky in the middle market. Shawn and Cheese are buying a house together rather than submitting to the sacrament of marriage. It's what many do. A house nowa-days is matrimony enough, at least for the young and affluent.

Old Edna Goodkind is defenseless against such people. Shawn and Cheese are represented by Brandi McCannon of Century 21, herself a kind of raunchy celebrity in Marin real estate, and like Shawn and Cheese morally vapid. The grocery carts at Safeway carry Century 21 ads displaying Brandi's image, a framed placard with her photo, coifed like an angelic country-western singer, photographed by a camera with Vaseline on the lens. No one knows Brandi McCannon's birth name; the catchy trochee-plus-dactyl she devised is her professional name, and she arrived in Marin wearing it, from the Orange County market. Now for seven or eight years running, Brandi McCannon has been Century 21's top-producing agent; she always wears all seven or eight lapel pins. Brandi is never burdened or distracted by irrelevant observations, neither to the left nor the right of her straight path to the 3 percent commission. She surely hasn't ever noticed a single thing about Edna Goodkind. To her, Edna Goodkind is only "the seller," or, moreover, "the elderly and infirm seller." For she will have noted that "the seller" needs to come away from the deal with $470,000. That's the low-end price of an apartment in Reward Village, where Edna hopes to spend her dying days. And all around that number, Brandi will have built her strategies.

My constant feeling is I'm sorry. I'm sorry that the Shawns and the Cheeses of the world take preeminence. For they do take preeminence, preeminence everywhere. It's the world. The Shawns and Cheeses climb up and stand upon the tip-top of the sorry little heap that is the world. They rear up like conquering iguanas in their pride. Also, it's probably too bad that I am the sort of man who, equipped with a negotiable personal appearance at last, is willing to postpone his client's welfare at the first opportunity on a beautiful morning in fall, and sacrifice Mrs. Goodkind for the sake of a flirtation, and leave the field open to Brandi.

Because I'm a truant now and liking it. I sometimes think this "sorriness" we religionists are taught to be so proud of (see above) might be all baloney. What if I'm *not* altogether sorry that the world is so fallen? It's how the world was founded, my dear Edna, upon sin. Only troublemakers raise the phony, insincere question of "the problem of evil," pretending it's a real question, pretending it points to a God who is maleficent or absent. Sin is the original form all our blessings took! Edna, at your advanced age you ought to have observed how tonic is anointment by sin, how delicious, and anyway how omnipresent, how fundamental is sin, to our very optics, our sensations, how indispensable in all kinesthesia, and seen it in yourself, too, and even gloried in it. You, too, Edna, must've been a beautiful baby. I've lately been led to wonder whether, during all those years in seminary and at my parish, if only I'd had a normal well-modeled lip, I might have never considered the priesthood. And never gotten started down that road. (The operation and the therapy, total this year, cost thirteen thousand dollars. I could have afforded that in 1990. Or 1980, for that matter. I could have taken out a loan even when I was a student.) The impediment of a harelip, in the end, really only *postponed* my inevitable vocation in avarice and pride and lust and all the rest. Or better, pride and lust and avarice and envy and everything were there all the time, driving me. During all my studies, while I pored over Ecclesiastes and Proverbs and Job and the Beatitudes and the Epistles, I was of course—while educating myself in virtue—educating myself in vice. I study the light but in order better to sculpt the dark.

So I'm out on my own recognizance today. I'm at large in San Rafael. Green Thumbs occupies the ground floor of an old commercial building on Fourth Street, a storefront, with a colorful childish handprint-decorated sign, a rectangle slapped everywhere by splayed fingers and palms. It's been there for years. I've been noticing it since long before there was a Thalia. I drove past the front, turned the corner, turned again into the alley, and as Thalia had directed me, I pulled up by the rear entrance to park my car—no longer the curate's unpretentious Toyota but the realtor's super-pretentious BMW, a necessary in the trade. It's white. White is a sterile ambulance color for a car, that's my own opinion; but white and platinum are the car colors recommended in in-service work-shops, and even touted recently by an article in Coldwell Banker's in-house magazine *Closing,* because white and platinum are colors clients associate with probity and solvency. No red allowed. Nor black, nor beige, nor the fine cranberry I'd prefer, nor the BMW forest green.

So I drove around back, and in the alley I came upon the parked Green Thumbs van, a big ten-seater for transport-ing developmentally disabled adults around town, its fenders and side panels decorated with those same handprints, as if big children had dipped wrist-deep in various paint pigments and then patted it all over. At the rear of the Green Thumb offices, the EMERGENCY EXIT ONLY doorway stood open to the alley sunshine. And there was one of her developmentally dis-abled adults, a richly freckled man whose mouth stayed open in a smile, rocking on the balls of his feet, while he watched me park my eighty-thousand-dollar car. Then Thalia appeared. I opened my door. And I got out and stood up, and we beheld each other, and I actually felt half entitled to be in love with her, an immense easy presumption, to absorb her unto myself, the way she smiled and the way she wore denim overalls, whose bib flattened her chest, and the way her hair had been modeled by a recent haircut into a shorter asymmetric brown bonnet with points at her cheeks.

Those bib overalls! Physical bodies are phenomena whose real *causes* (Aristotle, there) are outside our vision: we are bio-logical, physical figures, but also social and political figures, mystical apparitions, beasts, supposedly participants in the body of Christ, sexual icons, standing before each other. Thalia and I in the sun both knew how to collaborate in keeping the car between us, she filtering back toward the brown bricks of the wall, I standing up in the open, but behind my rear fender—so the threat of our hugging each other was never a question. Or even shaking hands. "John!" she said, with a sewing motion of her shoulder. "Yay!"

That cry of jubilation was also for the sake of her developmentally disabled adults, their morale. An offstage audience was collecting behind her in the doorway.

"Everybody? *John* is going to join us today."

As she spoke, then, she mooned toward me a look of hopeless apology. Because this was an even newer change in plans, which here she'd announced to me by bouncing it off everybody else. Oh, but she could have no idea how flexible I was willing to be, in any adventure, so long as it involved *her* and her short haircut and her blue denim OshKosh overalls, on this sunny day.

Developmentally disabled adults of several shapes and sizes had gathered in Green Thumbs' doorway, drawn by the spectacle.

Thalia confided to me across the distance, "Sandy will take over for the second half of the day. She had something she couldn't possibly break off. So she'll come up and rescue us after lunchtime. It's awkward: are you willing to leave your car here? That would be best. And ride the Green Thumbs bus with us? And then we'll come back for it? I thought we'd stop and get a picnic for *us* at Whole Foods. You and I can have our little *déjeuner* on the grass in some shady bower, while others toil. These guys are fine, they have their lunches." By her tone, she was referring to a row of brown paper bags somewhere.

I made a throwaway gesture to show complete agreeability, but I ducked inside my rear-passenger door because maybe that French word *déjeuner* got to me, or the shady bower. While my head was in there I seemed, or pretended, to arrange things inside. A windshield-frost scraper on the floor needed to be picked up and then set down again. An erect seatbelt buckle needed to be neatly tugged and twisted. The new Multiple Listing printout was on the backseat, and it needed to be tucked away inside the big spiral-bound street map of the county. From here on out, my gaze would be sheathed, for this is a typical male concession, to politeness, an all-important politeness, because I was like a heat-seeking missile. I would prevent my vision from focusing, all day in Thalia's company, and today my eyes would be dazed recording devices only, dead to immediate sight. Then at some point much later, in my own home, alone, in my solitude, and my sanity, I might reconstruct the afternoon and its spectacle under the Napa sun, that fomenter of illusions and enthusiasms. For the bib overalls I was filled with gratitude. For she is modest. The catechism's nice language, on the practice of forswearing the world's obscenity, expresses it thus (wherein this word *mystery* isn't just the intrigue of the flirt but a metaphysical immanence):

> Modesty protects the mystery of persons
> and their love.

A normal social, sexual being will have a tendency (a not-monstrous tendency, a rather purely pragmatic tendency) to revert to thoughts of specific inevitabilities, defended by heavy denim, at the double-stitched crotch there where the neat denim placket descends to nowhere. There are unavoidables in human society. Certain of these unavoidables, and the encounter with them, may be the aims for which "society" was invented in the first place—so it is that society is an arena for failure. Its little daily commonplace tournaments are instituted mostly to conduce to plenty of personal extinctions, a great abundance of extinctions, yet society treats them lightly as if they were jokes or little passing annoyances. That word *déjeuner* of hers seemed—pointedly, purposely—to evoke the Manet painting *Le Déjeuner sur l'Herbe;* everybody knows the painting, it shows artistic-looking Parisians lying around in a grove picnicking, but with a blandly defiantly unclothed woman. In the circle of folding chairs in Recovery Group at the clinic, "serious relationship" was the circumlocution that stood for the loss-of-virginity deed, and in those discussions I had come to *believe*—or maybe just hope—that Thalia was a virgin, like me. Our both being virgins would complicate the threat of some anatomical incompatibility, which we might confront that weekend, or even, also, somehow mercifully make it comedic. My own virginity was, at least, not worsened by ignorance, because I've seen plenty of the new kind of porn and have some idea of the kinds of things people are up to. But innocence, if that were Thalia's condition—that is, if it were true *ignorance*—might create a very awkward obstacle. I was aware that, still, my face was blazing, still thrust inside my car—(only because she'd used a French word, Lord!)—and I pulled out the MLS printout again, to iron out a dog-eared page, and reinsert it in the street map book, unwilling to reappear for a minute, because surely her allusion to an erotic painting couldn't have been totally accidental. Everybody knows that painting, and she's a sophisticated (if possibly innocent) woman. Or, if it wasn't an intentional allusion, it would have been "unintentional." Which, in my book, is as good as intentional.

She concluded, "Anyway!" in a happy, loud, gathering tone, because she was addressing everyone, the whole congeries of developmentally disabled adults who had flowed out through the door to collect in the sunshine, to behold the famous Mr. Gegenuber, the nice man who had come to be a fellow passenger today with them in their slapped-all-over bus.

The assembled clients—the preferred word—were interesting to meet at last, and oddly lovable, as is always the case with the retarded. I've known plenty of developmentally disabled adults, I've even worked with them on brief occasions, and I don't know why I should always find it so surprising: in an assembly of the developmentally disabled, the atmosphere is not chaos, not childish anarchy, but civility and tender consideration—more civility than among so-called normal students of a comparable mental age. It's the *normal* obstreperous ones who will foment a little riotousness wherever they can, exploiting any chink that admits a little sunshine, for example an emergency-exit-only door left ajar, leading to an alley. These so-called clients regarded me with a respect and genuine amiability, if with a few tics or squints. One middle-aged fellow stood habitually on tiptoe. Another, a woman, scratched both elbows at once, in a manner that was clearly compulsive. Everybody wore loose plastic vests of Day-Glo orange, standard-issue for their gardening work. The purpose of the vests, as I would later learn, was not just to prevent pedestrian accidents when they were working around a roadside. It was, even more, that the clients would be easier to find, in case they went off exploring in somebody's shrubbery.

Thalia told the assembly, her palms splayed open in air as if ready to pat their imprint on a new surface, "Everybody? Mr. Gegenuber is my friend!"

This got almost no response. I had the impression they'd already been given such basic information. They'd probably been discussing me already that morning, the friend of the teacher, who would be a guest on their bus. The only response was from one client, a youngish man, better postured than the rest but also wearing a plastic vest; he narrowed his eyes sarcastically at the news that I was a friend, a gesture aimed at my appreciation, meaning to indicate he wasn't a complete dope like these others here. He wanted to be considered exceptional, among his friends, the one with some brains. I got the feeling he would be the one with a bad attitude. (If only, back in the Garden, God had managed to keep us all developmentally disabled. It seems to have been his original plan. We might all be like the others here trusting their shepherdess. The single smart one was clearly going to be the problem.)

Meanwhile there were introductions. The names flowed by fast, and my ears were sound-muffled in the belief that I wouldn't really need to remember anybody's name. This is Tim. This is Susan. This is Veevee. This is George. And so forth. Everybody, this is John Gegenuber.

"We have Bosco *tomorrow*," I was scolded, rather sharply, by the one called George, the thin, red-haired one with a wealth of freckles.

"George loves Bosco," Thalia explained. I'd never heard of Bosco, and she said, "Didn't you have Bosco? As a child? It's a chocolate syrup. For putting in milk."

Just to hear Bosco described made George, with anticipation, grind his palms hard together and smile fiercely. I had to admit I'd never tasted Bosco, but I loved picturing Thalia as a child loving Bosco, probably wearing a similar, smaller edition of the same OshKosh overalls. She started revolving in place, "Has everybody peed?" This meant it was time for all to uproot themselves from the pavement and move toward the van.

George took the opportunity to tell me again, "Tomorrow is Bosco," and I could tell he liked me and was going to confide all his friendship in me, and it was a relief, to have made my first friend. It was clear that his disposition was always ferociously sunny and warm and confident; he was one of the fixed squinters.

I told him, "Maybe I've never had Bosco, but I can believe it's delicious." As a child I must have seen television commercials. One dimly remembers a clown on the label. And a squat glass jar. With a pump dispenser on top. I asked George, "You press down and it squirts, right?" It so satisfied him, to hear Bosco discussed, that he stayed silent and smiled but kept his mouth closed as if chocolate syrup filled it.

"I hate that," said a very short woman with a pointy nose, the one who had been scratching her elbows. She had been following the Bosco discussion with hatred that was visible, and she turned away, scratching more furiously.

"Miss Kunst? Miss Kunst?" voices had begun beseeching her, following her. From the two or three identifiable fussbudgets, there were a number of demands *(can I ride in the very back seat, can I sit by you, can I go home, why doesn't she have to wear a sweater)*. Now finally I had heard Thalia's last name. It was a name I would have remembered, an unfortunate name especially as it was pronounced generally by all her admirers at Green Thumbs. And of course, one's first thought is, there's a traditional, old-fashioned legitimate way of changing a name, if she should choose to. I, suitor and interloper and contestant to be the one who changes that name, removed myself from the tumult that spilled around her, for Thalia was the fountain of everyone's joy, the beacon of everyone's hope, the origin of justice. I had long since come out from behind my big white car, because after an interval it starts to feel decent to expose the whole figure while still keeping a distance. Thalia clearly felt as I did, keeping her own distance, and I recognized gratitude there. When I used to counsel people in their marriages (plenty of pre-marriage counsel, as well as mid-marriage, and a huge amount of post-), I found myself eventually making a peculiar observation about the whole quaint institution of society's bundling people off in permanent lifelong pairs. The securest marriages seem to be based on a certain shared *alienation*—as if marriage were an institution not for "entering into" society but for escaping it together, setting up a separate outpost. It's the "you-and-me-against-the-world" bond. It makes marriage innovative as an institution, culturally. It also makes each family peculiar. People trying for the norm are always splitting and regrouping and splitting again. Anyway, I thought I'd wander over to the van. Maybe help her out by encouraging a general motion in that direction.

Hands-in-pockets: it's one of the tried-and-true habitual attitudes of a clergyman, demonstrating affability and condescension. Parked beside the van was a trailer, loaded with lawn mowers and tarps and bristling with the handles of gardening implements. But it wasn't joined to the trailer hitch of the van. So apparently we wouldn't need it today. The van was one of the long kind, big enough to carry us all. By my count, there were seven developmentally disabled adults. One of them, a young woman, was hanging back near the building by the exit door, looking as if she were willing to be left behind, because she was simply so languid, as if she would in general prefer to be sitting. She was a pretty young woman—with, however, the characteristic wide-set, shallow-set eyes, the eyes of one too open to the world—and she seemed to be pregnant. Her body was so constructed that I couldn't tell for sure. It wasn't her belly, so much, that warned me; it was her stance, her sea legs, and how her spine was planted in her pelvis. Her shiny brown hair had been combed back from a middle parting and secured with plastic barrettes, so I had to think of a mother somewhere in Marin this morning, dressing her grown-up daughter with care and driving her down here to drop her off for her day's work. If this were in fact a pregnancy, what would the girl's mother do, in becoming a grandmother? Especially if, too, a grandchild might be similarly retarded? Well, she could simply show courage and raise the baby, prolonging her years of child raising, and even (with a little fortitude, and a little insight) feel that she was lucky in her whole situation. Best possible way to imagine it. Or, who knows, if it were born defective, a grandmother might rather just find a "nice place" to send it away, and be free of it. That would be more the Marin style. It's one of the millions of nuanced reasons why Marin County keeps its sparkle and why values are holding, while other areas have pretty much crashed lately in the big down cycle.

The clients all knew the routine, and all seven were sifting into the van, with the exception of the pregnant one, who seemed happy enough where she was. Also George the Bosco fan hung back, alone, picking at the buckles on his backpack to get inside it. George's prominent elbows were always outthrust, in any activity he undertook, and I recognized there the kind of personality I favor, a man with an unselfconscious avidity. I even identify with the way George spends half his time lifting on his tiptoes; he's so zealous about whatever's coming up next. It's what I'm always doing, inside myself, though personal dignity makes me hang back. If I were back in grade school, George would be my friend. "Not now, George," said Thalia, because she seemed to know what he was up to. "If you eat it all on the trip, you won't have anything left for lunchtime," she chanted. I recognized in George, also, a glutton like myself, fellow sinner, never overweight but always jealously voracious. Flat-footed now, he surrendered the backpack to Thalia, who took it from him and zipped it back together and restored it, reversed, to his embrace.

She raised her voice, "Does everybody have their backpack?"

So we were making progress, and I checked the face of my cell phone for the time. It was eleven thirty. I had promised to have a telephone conversation at one o'clock with Brandi McCannon and Edna, who would both be at Edna's bungalow. The inspection was going to go on without me, so I wanted Edna at least to hear my voice. And feel reassured. Brandi McCannon, in my absence, would be there on the scene. There was something calculated—that is, something tactical—in asking for a new inspection at this point. Brandi, as buyers' agent, wasn't required to explain why she wanted a new inspection. She had made it clear, too, that she didn't intend to explain. I was uneasy about it because—knowing Edna Goodkind as I do—she might actually be a little alarmed if total strangers rang her doorbell today and I wasn't there. She might be confused. I wanted at least my voice to be present on the phone, the old black Bakelite phone in her hallway in her bungalow, while the strange tall "inspector" man with the tool belt tramped up and down in her house, jabbing a screwdriver at window sashes, climbing into the attic above, donning a jumpsuit to go down in the crawl space below. On Monday, furthermore, I would drop by in person and have a cup of tea with Edna. I knew my plan today was unprofessional—to try to be *virtually* present at the inspection, while speaking by cell phone from inside the traveling Green Thumbs bus, or standing out in the Civic Center gardens with our laborers-under-the-sun. As I climbed into the van's passenger side, this all felt like being an adolescent again, all this irresponsibility. But also—this, too, adolescent!—it felt like love, doomed as love, unwise and other-worldly and sticky as love. The woman in the OshKosh coveralls with the pixie-style haircut was a mysterious creature, strange as a mermaid or some alien squid offering herself most delicately, cautiously, formally, for my acquaintance.

So of course, just in getting out of town, my cell phone had to ring. The illicit aspect of the whole adventure—getting in the passenger seat beside her, while she turned the key and made the van roar, buckling my seat belt, checking on our jolly crew in back as they jostled or bickered—the day's illegitimate, piratical, truant aspect was exactly stung, exactly tagged, when my cell phone started singing in my jacket and BRANDI CENTURY 21 was displayed in the dim caller-ID window, deep in my pocket. The Green Thumbs van happened to be rising, gaining altitude and velocity on the entrance ramp, and I pulled out the phone out and flipped it open (more to cut off my loud "Night on Bald Mountain" ringtone than because I wanted to talk to Brandi McCannon) and I said, "Brandi! Hi! Are you ready to do business today?"

"Morning, John. We're at my office. I'll be glad when you can get here, dear, because we've got *plenn-ty* to discuss."

Some sarcasm there. Something had gone wrong.

"Aren't we still planning to phone-conference at one o'clock? At the moment I'm pretty busy."

"I want to explain something to you. The sellers are having a money problem."

"The sellers. Shawn and Cheese, you mean," I said, just to clarify, but more because I liked using those names whenever possible, just to rub Brandi's nose in it. "What kind of money problem are they having?"

"Can you come by? Sorry, dear heart, but you know, we had originally planned to meet in person."

BRANDI'S OFFICE IS north of Terra Linda, so it was in the same general direction we were headed. In this particular mall the storefronts are mostly the usual simple terrariums around a parking lot, so the Century 21 building stands out as unique: it's a small castle, with a crenellated parapet and a pointy tower, standing on its own island in the center of the parking lot. The upper story is empty façade, with battlements and four pennants that don't hang limp but stand out stiffly, as if they were snapping in the wind, because they're molded of hard plastic.

I asked Thalia to park our hilarious van at a distance from the castle. The slightest appearance of being unbusinesslike would put me at a disadvantage with Brandi. Brandi, on the phone, had seemed to feel *herself* now at some obscure disadvantage, but she's very good at what she does; she will always have found a way to put a perceived disadvantage to some clever leverage. Thalia brought us to anchor beside a landscape island, at a middling distance from the Century 21 castle, where our isolation made us perhaps more conspicuous in the carnival van, as the whole lot was mostly empty. Anyway I got out and spoke through the open window, "I promise this won't take long," and I hopped the high curb of the landscape island. Which was really just a sunken well of soil. On its single new, bare sapling, a yellow ID tag was clipped to a twig. It read TREE (DECIDUOUS).

Of course Brandi had seen me coming, from her lookout in her castle. The swinging glass door flashed as she came out to intercept me, carrying what looked like a counteroffer, its pages flipping and pinwheeling in the parking-lot breeze, her high heels clicking, her body in her buttoned wool suit as it advanced to confront me very feminine yet somehow football-player-like, as if female secondary sex characteristics were a paradoxical form of armor. She'd come out to intercept me outside for this realtor-to-realtor parley because (this would be standard wisdom, and a matter of routine) she wanted to limit any contact of mine with her clients Shawn and Cheese, who were visible inside. I could see them through the big plate-glass window. Sitting in those upholstered chairs, they looked like they'd been called in to the principal's office for discipline. They had that slouch.

As a realtor, I've always preferred the middle-market and the first-time-buyers—rather than the bigger commissions in the "high-end" market—because of what's at stake, spiritually. In the high end, the house-hunting game can be all too often bedeviled by unexamined motives, maybe even unmentionable motives, or mysterious unfathomable motives. Certain people really don't want to think about their true reasons for buying a house, especially as they get rich enough that necessity and pure happenstance are no longer limits. It's a mystery, buying a new home. It's a ceremony. Home—particularly the little personal skit of "buying" and taking "ownership" of it—is always (for all of us, whether high or low, whether wise or foolish) a plunge into absolutely imaginary quantities—money, love, the future, our ostensible selves—all such fluid and evaporative glimmerings that can vanish at the moment we arrive there. We seek our reflection while we're in the world—we seek to know our own image—and so we conjure up around ourselves great shining clouds of real estate, among other attainments. I personally don't have the stomach for walking people through a multi-million-dollar house only because buying it provides a way for them to accomplish some remote vindication or pretend there is no such thing as death or distract themselves from lovelessness. Shawn and Cheese may have been shopping in the middle market, but in their case, a house was to replace marriage. They would have believed that love would always bind them together, sweet love, the kind sung about in songs on the radio, love antecedent to any formal exchange of vows. But, at a certain wonderful stage of life, maybe "love" is still mostly just sex and excellent restaurant meals. What Shawn and Cheese would be missing in their new house is the education that comes of having sacramentally (that would mean, without anyone's "understanding" it) acknowledged that their love has been underwritten, like a loan, by a much larger love, that there exists a love so great, such an ocean of luminance, of which they are the merest fizz, a love so original, so infinite and incomprehensible, that they have light years to traverse together before they will come to the dimmest guess of its source. Or even suspect that such a sea of love might exist.

"Here's a little bit of good news for you," said Brandi, stopping at her personal scrimmage line, planting her feet. "You've got me by the balls."

The strategies of Brandi McCannon are always many layered. "Well, that is good news," I said—agreeably, too!—without the slightest irony or subversive humor. A constant principle at work, here, is that I'm not as smart as Brandi McCannon. This isn't an attitude of defeatism, it's simply a fact, and a pertinent circumstance in my own planning: any relative weakness of mine in our comparative natural gifts is a useful consideration. To speak more fairly, I'm just not as ardent. Not as dedicated. My job doesn't keep me up at night. A realtor, like anybody who practices a skill, has to understand his own deficiencies and strengths and not be unrealistic. Brandi McCannon—all Marin knows this—is able to play a kind of hardball far above most people's abilities, even renowned old realtors' abilities. She has changed the scene here in Marin, over a decade. This morning, facing her in a parking lot in my astigmatism—somehow fatally *weakened* by the presence of Thalia at my back—all I could hold on to was that I had "right" on my side. I was on the side of justice. I had Edna Goodkind to protect, her cobwebby collection of menorahs, her living room card tables holding towers of books, her ichthyology magazines illustrating ancient extinct marine mollusks and giant squids, her dead brown hydrangeas in a vase, (all this anyway before I cleared the place for staging it, leaving Edna in cleaner rooms awaiting evacuation herself). I said, "Tell me, what is the advantage I have over you?"

"My kids took their own money."

I thought perhaps I *did* know what she meant. But I just stared at her, to make her suffer a little, and explain further.

"The loan can't fund. Part of the down payment was going to be an inheritance? Shawn got an inheritance? From an uncle who died? Then they did some tricky stock market maneuver they can't get out of. So the money's not there. They took it. And the lender is gone."

It was why they'd looked so contrite, sitting there inside the Century 21 waiting room on the Ethan Allen furniture. Brandi and I, out on the parking lot where we stood, were temporarily those kids' stand-in parents. For a hallucinatory, beatified instant I was wedded to Brandi McCannon, with an actual funny influx of warmth from somewhere, not just asphalt heat at midday.

She flopped her printed-out pages. "They want a ninety-day escrow. You *know* you don't have another offer. You'd be being sweet to the kids, letting them have time to get some money together."

Of course it was a likable notion, that the situation could be just that simple. But she seemed to have a kind of odd, other self-certainty, and there was a sneer in her smile. There would be mysteries folded in here. I didn't exactly understand it. Brandi's own insulting mysteriousness made her proud standing there, a buccaneer. I actually felt myself a failure already, my back turned to our colorful van, which was moored at a distance, my merry crew inside watching me.

"A long escrow of course would be a problem, you know, for us, Brandi. We would like to get into Reward Village. We don't want to wait forever. The seller, Edna, you know, she's studying the menus in the place. She *talks about* the menus at Reward Village. It's one of her favorite topics."

We did have no other offer. Corner lots move slow in Gerstle Park. But a ninety-day escrow seemed uncalled-for. I only wished I were back on the road with Thalia watching the countryside go past. Or lying out in a shady bower picnicking while her seven clients labored in the hedgerows. There could be a bottle of white wine, so I thought, silencing the usual quiet chime of wisdom. I'm a second-rate realtor, Lord, and what I wanted was to be pulling the cork, reclining on a lawn, releasing from the bottle the resinous chardonnay perfume (oak, pear, grapefruit), as I anticipated it, over the shady lawns of Dr. Auctor's estate. The Brandi McCannon who was smiling at me in the sun—and this is typical—uses the word REALTOR® in all her faxes and emails and letters, unfailingly, rather than realtor. It's more correct. This is something people in my own office go along with, too. Everybody seems to be doing it lately, in fact. The National Association of REALTORS® has actually *patented* for itself the English word! Or so it says, and it commands that it be rendered that way everywhere, caps and all. Brandi is the type to treat such a rule lovingly.

"How did they lose their money, exactly?"

"They didn't quite 'lose' it yet. Their friend has a start-up. They invested it, and now they can't liquidate it. They'll have to do a whole new loan app. So! Hey! We're out of escrow!" she concluded as if we'd landed on the luckiest outcome possible, holding up her arms, willing to be asked to dance, as we happened to be out on this open Monopoly board together. "Doesn't Reward Village have a rather lengthy waiting list?"

She knew perfectly well about their waiting list. She's been active in this county longer than I have. She reads the articles in the *Marin Independent Journal.* She knows about Reward Village. She knows, too, that I can't afford to gamble with Mrs. Goodkind's money. If the house has to go back on the market, it's going to be time to reduce the asking price. A ten- or twenty-thousand-dollar cut in price reduces Mrs. Goodkind's life choices in specific ways. She needs some money to live on, too. It could mean, for example, that her Reward Village apartment, when she gets one, will be one of the cheaper units on the north side, lacking a "balconette," which is not a balcony but just a ledge, really just a plastic railing outside a sliding door, an architectural feature too small even to stand on, but a few potted geraniums might squeeze into the space. A balconette is a slight thing, but a geranium does cheer a widow. Or, reducing her asking price means the living/dining area won't be big enough for Edna's upright piano, which she herself can't play, but which her sons play when they visit. Already she had been fretting over the high cost of piano movers.

"Reward Village is adding a new wing," I told Brandi. "Edna's particular apartment—the one she loves—is going to be available for just a certain slot of time when the construction is done. They'll all go on the market in November and she'll have to qualify, and it can get snapped up." As I spoke, I could see the powders fusing behind her blue eyes: she would get on the phone as soon as we quit talking, to speak to Reward Village administration, and maybe to the contractors, too, and get a construction-schedule estimate, just to check my story. It was likely she already knew about the new wing.

"Oh, that's a disappointment!" she cried, piteously, as if she were picturing the drama of "Edna Homeless," carrying a garbage bag in the night, wearing frayed bedroom slippers along dark B Street, in the neighborhood of her former bungalow. "I don't know what in the world we can do then, John." Her empathy actually dampened her eye and she clutched back her papers against her rib. The request for a ninety-day escrow seemed to be withdrawn. With grief she half-turned to look at her clients in the office window, stranded in there in the carpeted waiting area where there would be no entertainment for them but a *Wall Street Journal* and a *Marin I-J* on the coffee table.

"They're gonna be bummed," she said, watching her castle; then she turned back to me. "We'll get back to you and we'll all stay in touch on this, John. Always a pleasure." Her high heels started to skate slowly in reverse. She was being drawn backward, toward the fort. "Call me on your cell? Later today? During the inspection?" I was trying to let this vaguely bamboozled feeling well up and take a clearer shape. She continued to want a new inspection, even though the house was out of escrow now. It would have seemed rude of me to be openly suspicious and inquire into that barefaced logical contradiction.

Shawn and Cheese, I could see, were shrugging out of their wing chairs and coming outside. They'd seen Brandi glance back at them, and they thought they were being summoned.

I wanted to get away without an encounter, so I started backing away toward the van; and of course Brandi, as a pro, would want to prevent a meet-up. I said, "So your buyers still want the place reinspected. Although we're out of escrow." So maybe I would go ahead and seem suspicious, but the comment was intended only as a good-bye shot, not a real interrogation. That's how it bounced.

She said, also by way of farewell, "Hey, my kids are serious. We love that place. They'll get their money together. We'll be back."

But the castle's plate-glass door flashed again, and the happy couple was coming. A meet-up was going to happen. They were sweeping along on the open asphalt with no destination but us. Shawn, the male one—exactly like an Orthodox ikon, i.e., spoon-faced, pale, his sparse beard pubic-looking, but wearing sunglasses—flung out his arms wide and addressed us across the asphalt. "Hey, we fucked up!" he jeered, as they came on, his girl galumphing on her clunky fashionable shoes.

Brandi told me, "John, you know, you and I are on the same side. This was just a little bad communication. We can work around it."

"We're on the same side, Brandi," I confirmed. She meant, in the Making-People's-Dreams-Come-True sense. "Naturally, we'd both like a clean escrow."

"Here," she tottered forward and lunged across space, handing over the pages, "you can at least look this over, because we'll get back to you eventually. I'll hang out during the inspection. There have been some market adjustments. And a new comp in the neighborhood."

This was new. This could be why she seemed cheery about falling out of escrow. The "new comparable" was a house sale somewhere nearby. Either it had been low-balled at some reduced price, so a new appraisal of Edna's nice corner-lot bungalow would lower her asking price, or else—and this was the likelier possibility with someone like Brandi—the new comp might be high and would *raise* the appraised value of Edna's house. In that case, Brandi would be capable of betraying her clients' interest to arrange a bigger commission for herself.

Shawn and Cheese arrived. Cheese is overweight but she wore grey elastic tights that conformed to a vertical crease at her pudenda's little nibbling, and black patent-leather boots big as clown shoes. I said, "Brandi, I'll take a cut in the offer if these two get, like, married. I mean it. That would be my condition. Church wedding. I'm totally serious. Condition of sale."

It was a joke. But it was a weird joke, and a mean, flippant joke, born from a spasm, if a rather satisfying spasm. The regrettable remarks, in life, are always the kind where there's satisfaction and it feels good.

The insanity of it was evident in Brandi's recoil and her little rattle of incredulity. It was an unbusinesslike thing to say and would increase her advantage. She modified her incredulity, to a slightly cracked expression, a slightly pleased expression, as if I'd personally insulted her. "John, what a cute idea! I'll absolutely write that into the offer," she said. "Come on, you guys," she told her clients.

The rock star was delighted. He might have lingered to hear more, but he was being pulled by the elbow back to the castle. "He's fucking nuts," he said with a fresh admiration.

WHILE THALIA DROVE, I flipped through the offer, but I didn't focus on it; I just wanted the pages as a place to press my hectic face into. That had been a stupid outburst. It was unprofessional. Nobody in this van had heard it, but I was ashamed among them anyway. As for the offer, there was no reason for me to look at it. There was no reason for Brandi to have given it to me at all. It was wastepaper I'd been handed, and I slid it up on the dashboard and I flipped open my phone, to call Edna at home, to make that old black telephone ring in the hallway, and get her out of her chair, summon her from the house's musty recesses, dingy beiges and lavender dusts, gangrenous cooking smells. Brandi, in her Century 21 castle, later today, would no doubt be pressing PRINT on a new document, having changed a few numbers. It's what realtors do.

On the fifth ring Edna answered, with her antique sweetness. She always lifts the onerous receiver to her ear with a duck of the head as if she were about to be let in on a wonderful secret from the outside world. I told her that an inspector would be visiting today, just like the other inspector she might remember, the one who came last month. This new inspector was just going to have another routine look at the house—and not to worry because the buyers were paying for this inspection—and I told her she ought to remember about this, because we'd discussed it the day before. But I wouldn't be there. Of course Brandi McCannon would be there. Edna loves Brandi. Everybody loves Brandi.

Edna reacted with a little bit of dismay. She has motherly feelings toward me, and she'd wanted me to be there; she'd thought of the occasion today as a party. She has an old box of chalky cookies which she enjoys arranging on a plate for guests, and then there's always the whole topic of ichthyology to unpack—which is always a dead end, because she is the first to say she doesn't understand any of that anymore, though it was very important at the time, involving her husband's ground-breaking research into the mechanics of reproduction between mollusks in the mud at the bottom of the sea. Talking about her husband and passing the cookies are the best parts of selling a house. At her age she feels, on the one hand, that $570,000 is way too much money—obscenely too much for anyone to pay, especially a young couple—for her little old bungalow, yet on the other hand she worries, in a vague arithmetical way, about the expense of getting into Reward Village. She can't understand why her rosebushes don't add to the appraised value. She bade me good-bye mewing, "Whatever you say, sweetheart," and I folded my phone and stuffed it away. She makes that word *sweetheart* sound like Yiddish, saddling me with filial responsibilities I can scarce analyze stirring way back in the Old Testament. The vanishing cow pastures of north Marin flew past the car window. After I'd folded the cell phone over the voice of Edna, the developmentally disabled adults were allowed to talk again, as Thalia had asked them to be polite and not speak during my phone conversation. Everyone, all seven developmentally disabled adults, had watched my agent-to-agent parley in the parking lot outside the papier-mâché castle, through the van windows. While they watched (with a sudden new loyalty to me!) they had reached a few conclusions about Brandi, from observing our body language together. Susan, a pale, red-haired woman sitting messily on the van's second seat bench, who made the general impression of a Raggedy Ann doll, said only, "She's mean." This wasn't a moral evaluation; it was an objective, cool, business-ethics evaluation: it meant simply that Susan would prefer not to do business with Brandi McCannon. Tony, a good-looking one with an alluring light in his eye, whose only outward sign of a mental deficiency was a strange raw grin, seemed mostly impressed by Brandi's beauty. I hadn't heard him say a word during the entire morning, until we started pulling out of the parking lot. He was excited. "She is a fox. That woman is a babe. She is foxy. You can tell. You can tell all about her, just by looking. That woman? Shish. Bam. Woman like that. Bam. Know what I mean? Bam."

Thalia, while she drove, caught my eye, angling an eyebrow indicating that, in Tony, this was more than just talk. Indicating that our friend Tony could be a real problem.

"Tell me something," I spoke in a low tone to Thalia's golden ear, my cleric's warm delicacy, pitching my voice quieter than the engine sound, "Is that one pregnant?"

Immediately I regretted the pronoun "that one," as one might point out a beast among other beasts. The language surrounding developmentally disabled adults, even at its most stilted and correct, keeps slipping naturally into discourtesy. Professionals who, every day, work with them and get frustrated with them and love them, are entitled to discuss them with less euphemism. That was my experience long ago, when I used to volunteer with the Special Olympics. And Thalia, on our two evenings together so far, was funny on the topic of the clients' foibles and buffooneries. Mishaps with clothing. Amusing misunderstandings of common speech. One of her clients, when entrusted with a lawn mower, invariably heads out to mow down the nearest flowerbeds and is an enemy of all flowerbeds everywhere. She says the staff at Green Thumbs refers to the place as All Thumbs.

"Francesca, yes, you guessed it," she said, speaking of the pregnant one. "And yes," she glanced with the same cautionary leer that had referred to Tony, "maybe you guessed. It's him. She's due this month. She doesn't look it, sturdy girl. She's having a Caesarean in a couple of weeks."

"Tony? Is the father?"

"Knocked her up. Bit of a scandal, of course, around Green Thumbs."

"My gosh, how did that happen?"

"John, it happened in the usual way. In this case, in the bushes."

The thought that shifted inside (while remaining safely, deeply buried) was Thalia could nevertheless be a virgin. She could be knowledgeable and even use a flip tone but, yet, be as inexperienced as I am. What came out of my mouth of course was the wise calm inquiry, "I hope the two lovers' *parents* were forgiving."

"Everyone has been wonderful," she said, marveling, suspending skepticism.

Talking in the front seat was discreet; there was so much noise, the whap of wind in the partly open side vents, and a new sound of humming, or singing, from one of the clients in back, a middle-aged male bass alternating between two deep notes, contentedly.

"It happened on my watch," said Thalia. "They slipped away together while we were in the Civic Center park. The place we're headed now. The whole park is big enough, there are plenty of places to sneak off. As you have seen, the fellow is a great big Lothario. And Francesca is cute. And I'll tell you something: the grandparents in question have nothing to worry about." She glanced across at me. It was a moment when I'd torn my gaze from her, from the admiration of her amazing female shoulder as it shrugged sometimes in her monologue. I've seen plenty of shoulders in my life, we've all seen plenty of shoulders, but I suppose Thalia's now was particularly numinous because I'd begun to hope or believe that it might soon be mine. I would own it, and have custody of it, possession, ownership, proprietorship, as with real estate; I might someday have care of it, responsibility for it. "Genetically, Tony and Francesca are both 'mutes,' as we call them. Meaning"—her voice went lower—"the baby will be phenotype normal. They did an amniocentesis, just to be sure. But the whole thing is lucky. In both cases, with the grandparents on both sides, they're all young enough and had no other children. They're all willing to be 'up' for this."

Her mouth was a little pursed then as she paid attention to the traffic. When that lip and mine met, on that night standing in her doorway, the two sensitive surfaces only lay against each other; we didn't chew and enmouth each other as actors in movies do, though surely, we've both lived long enough to see plenty of dramatic kissing on the big screen—all during the eighties, the nineties, into the new millennium, actors kissing passionately, only to be replaced by a new generation of actors kissing passionately, while fashions changed, sideburns went in and out of style, variations on women's figures went in and out of style, and mega movie stars came into celebrity and went out of celebrity, and we ourselves rose through awkward decades, observing the styles of kissing onscreen. Instead, our two mouths, products of Dr. Auctor's brightly lit chamber of anesthesia, stayed immobile and tangent, experimentally for a minute, and not only because of the natural paralysis of self-consciousness, but also because the two masks will have to go very slowly in discovering the soul. It was actually a childish moment. We both knew it.

She went on, "So, you see. There'll be these two grandmothers now who are going to *compete* over who gets to spend time with the grandchild. However," she raised that same eyebrow, "just keeping a like-chaperone-surveillance on Tony is part of the job today. He's a 'Love Machine.' He's 'Catnip to the Ladies.'"

I smiled but kept watching the highway. One keeps one's eyes out ahead. A highway is a drink for the eyes. In a highway, as it wells up from the central vanishing point, there arises always an immediate future; the pour keeps healing, healing the central open sore in the world. It's purled from the parched colors all around, colors of pavement, colors of freeway sound wall, of roadside cinders, all the landscape expanding around the mysterious origin point in the middle of the horizon, from which emerges the road, the road bleeding away from Eden, the road itself the only consolation, the road outward into disappointment and—these are all the world's consolations, this is all the advice I might somehow communicate to a son if I had one, about keeping one's eyes on the road ahead for what certainties man is vouchsafed—disappointment, death of course, and self-reliance.

THE CIVIC CENTER park is a ten-minute drive, though we did stop for gas, and we stopped at a delicatessen for lunch provisions and, yes, a bottle of wine. A ten-dollar Oregon Pinot Gris. Smoked chicken. A chilled escargot dish she knew about. Asparagus in sesame. Crackers and a hard cheese. It might be a meal we would reminisce about over the decades. While we were in the store, the developmentally disabled adults could be trusted to stay in the van, they're such a conformist, Pharisean flock, all policing each other closely. One funny thing neither of us mentioned: the crackers on the checkout conveyor belt. Crackers would have provoked, in an *un*repaired palate, a lot of nasopharyngeal "snicking" (as we call it), snicking being an eating habit particular to cleft palates, audible, if muffled. It's the reason oatmeal used to be my nemesis. Indeed all breakfast cereals. The horror of Raisin Bran. But there in the deli neither of us mentioned any of this or, possibly, even let it cross our minds; we just paid, while in white cardboard cartons the most delicious things we could think of rode past on the rubber conveyor belt at the checkout stand, us standing there, for all the world betrothed by our radiant credit card.

The van, whenever we were on the road moving, stayed remarkably quiet inside. The docility of mentally retarded adults—the gregarious ability to sit still and be so patient, and just wait for the next thing—must be a kind of restraint they've learned from having made a few embarrassing, awful mistakes. A few bad judgments of their own, a few penalized initiatives, will probably be stingingly memorable and will have taught them it's better to stay put, Day-Glo vest or no Day-Glo vest, better just to be patient and not even move around at all, until directions come from a Miss Kunst or from some other one of the superior race. They will know that, as a group, they are inferior in wisdom and understanding, sticking together in their little crew. The one thing they need to know is that somebody loves them. That's their ticket.

Thus our traveling van, patted with handprints in green and red and blue and orange, stayed mostly quiet inside while we were on the road. One interruption in the serenity is always George. He felt compelled to announce every few minutes that he would be drinking Bosco tomorrow, turning to speak loudly in the ear of his seatmate Susan (the Raggedy-Ann-dressed woman, the one who disapproved of Brandi McCannon). Susan had no response at all to George, as if she literally couldn't hear him or were just very tolerant. This Susan is an interesting case. She is an investor, and a successful one. Thalia told me as we drove that she picks mutual funds and she does a little better than the averages. She shows every outward sign of being intelligent—she actually has a kind of dignity, out of keeping with her baby-doll outfit—but then she also seemed to think that Brandi McCannon *lived in* the Century 21 building, that the plaster Disneyland castle in a parking lot was Brandi's home. Susan's father has to place the mutual fund orders, and he keeps the records for her, but she makes the decisions. So obviously part of her brain is working, and she's having a little fun. In any case, she suffered George's blaring boasts in her ear with such aplomb as if she existed in a separate dream alongside George's.

The other source of noise, eventually, was an unfortunate match of seatmates at the very back of the bus: Oscar and Veevee. Oscar was a middle-aged bald man who made it an active policy

in life to be envious of anything anybody else had. He envied
Veevee's window seat. He envied George's guarantee of Bosco
and, later, George's acquisition of somebody else's granola bar.
He envied Susan's big account at Fidelity. (All this according to
Thalia.) He envied a jacket belonging to his other seatmate, Tony.
He even envied me: I got to sit next to the beloved Miss Kunst
up front.

All his complaints of injustice seemed to drive his neighbor
Veevee mad. Veevee was the elbow-scratcher. When I turned
to see, she was pale and red-nostriled in fury, jerking her head
away to aim her very small beak out toward the whole world or
up at the van's ceiling. Wherever *he* wasn't. On her lap, in exas-
peration she kept lifting and repiling her hands, as if she were
folding and refolding an invisible tangled fabric there. When
we pulled into a gas station for a fill-up, she called out, "Miss
Kunst?" and she shot up from her seat to open the side door and
present herself at the driver's-side window, standing outside in
front of the gas pump.

"What is it, Veevee?" said Thalia. It was rare for one of the
sheep to bolt from the order.

She checked back at Oscar, and so did I. Oscar was older
than I, his cheeks unshaven, his eyes perpetually panicked, his
hairline receding deeply like an intellectual's. He said, "How
come Veevee gets to go outside?"

Thalia turned back to Veevee, sensing something more serious here, and said, "What did he do?"

Veevee only rolled her eyes. In her chagrin she was rubbing
her ear with an inner wrist, and then her entire forearm started
sawing at the ear. She has the sort of face that narrows to a point
in the middle. Her close-set eyes, her little peach pit of a chin,
her lipless mouth, everything focused toward the nose, a sensitive nose, raw with readiness to be offended. I got the feeling that
pretty much everything was offensive to Veevee: nothing ever
quite measured up. This nuisance of a fellow passenger wasn't her
only irritation. It was one of a lifelong multitude of irritations in

a well-rehearsed disposition to rage. At last, her forearm rubbing her neck, she said, "Tony did something."

So the problem wasn't Oscar, it was Tony, and Thalia didn't need to hear any more. It had been a sexual impoliteness. Thalia let herself out and went straight around back, to enter by the side door and sit down beside Tony (he of the enviable jacket, a handsome young man in his twenties) and speak quietly in his ear. She talked in a whisper, but a forceful whisper, while Tony only smiled, looking forward out the window, beaming. Then she took him by the wrist: she lifted his limp hand from the seat and planted it firmly on his own knee, pressing it down, to cement it there.

I got out to fill the car with gas. Thalia had passed me the Green Thumbs credit card to feed to the slot in the pump. Nobody needed to go to the bathroom; everybody had gone, prudently, when we were back at the Green Thumbs office. The van, a Ford, drank thirty gallons and soon we were on the road again, and Thalia said, "The Civic Center will only take an hour. Sandy will relieve us and we'll be free. For our little hedonistic dalliance in the wine country." With *that* remark, while yet keeping her eye on the road, she made a glimmer in my direction. And I'm such a villain, just as wicked as Tony: for a disturbing instant (in my little imagination only) Thalia seemed to flash as a mink of very sharp tooth. Did she know what she was saying? Of *dalliances* and *hedonism*, surely she was speaking inside quotation marks, savoring the cliché. It's of course a common style of facetious humor. But everything seemed so eroticized, quotation marks always a strip tease. Maybe an old male celibate is oversensitive, compared to the rest of this rubbed-numb society, but how can people say electrifying things so easily? The ostensible innocence of women is an open question. In all my experience women are much more alert than men in these matters, more insightful, more nuanced. Or ought to be. As a minister of two decades I've seen a lot of human nature, and I've observed it in both genders. How can they be blind to it? Or innocent of it? Or pretend to be? It's really a torment. They actually seem not to notice what they're doing. So it is that men are consigned to live in an evil hypocrisy and actually get comfortable in it as if they were stupid. Only this morning, on my computer screen the actual blaze of the goddess in all her terrible power rose in that sourceless fountain. Such a goddess had nothing to do with the person incarnated beside me. Yet I was *unashamed* of my sordid secret life, totally unashamed, like some serial rapist sitting there. That goddess had of course fled before the actual Thalia, fled instantly, to mythological mists. Such rudiments of life keep getting exposed for the male's nose to be rubbed in.

"His real name is Hieronymus," she mused as she drove. She was going back to the subject of Dr. Auctor. "At the clinic, the name tag says DR. B. AUCTOR. Have you noticed? And Dwayleen calls him Bim. So does Madonna. They both refer to him as Bim." (Dwayleen and Madonna are clinic nurses.)

I said, "I suppose if you've got a name like Hieronymus, you call yourself something else."

"Yeah, but he's really *rich*," she retorted. It was a non sequitur, and a pleasant non sequitur, the kind of thing that, if we were married, I would love to encounter, in the mornings over coffee, or in the evenings at a restaurant table, or while driving home together from some social occasion—it was pleasing because it wasn't an entirely illogical non sequitur; there was an aroma at the rim. "You imply there's something nefarious. About being rich."

In the seat behind us, George declared loudly in wonderment, "Hieronymus Bosco," and he made a short laugh, having discovered an esoteric funny connection in the world for himself, an elusive sequitur in *his* world taking shape.

Thalia said, "I'll tell you about his medical accreditation," entering upon the story, as she'd got it from Margot, of Dr. Auctor's previous life in New York thirty years ago. According to Margot, as a young physician he didn't affiliate with a hospital to serve his residency. Which would have been the normal thing.

He financed his own clinic with his own money, and he bought his own equipment, and he hired his own nurses and anesthesiologist and staff and whatever.

I made the same point as before. "Well, people are allowed to be rich. It's not against the law."

"Then he never charged fees of his patients either, all his first patients. He was giving away plastic surgery for free, mostly to a destitute immigrant population he'd go out and *get*. Like, *find*. Or non-English-speaking types. He would go *to* people. Go out and get them and offer, and do it for free."

"Like, charitably."

"He wasn't doing beautification, supposedly; it was birth defects and injuries. So it seems. But that was how he served his required residency. He hired legitimate doctors at his own clinic and he *found* patients."

"Presumably he does have a degree."

"From a school in Hyderabad, India. Which you can see on his wall at the clinic. It's up there. Have you ever been in his office? The diploma is on the wall. It says 'blah-blah-blah Hyderabad, India.'"

"You are a snoop."

"I told you. It's Margot." This spoken with a grim rue, for Margot's complications of personality. Only an obsessive like Margot would have done all this footwork.

I added a passing, relevant sigh—of sorriness, for the Margot situation, and her little nip with suicide. I have some sympathy. In my case, after surgery erased the red seam traveling from lip to nostril, I did experience a few slight brushes with a sort of meaninglessness. All my life, that foremost blemish had been essential to me. I'd *used* it. I'd built around it. In high school, in college, in seminary. As a realtor. And before realty, as a minister. During the days when I gave sermons, I consciously employed the snerfling. *Hallown me nhy name. Ngim us nhis nay our nayly mren.* I never put in my obturator, on Sundays or ever. The reader doesn't need to know what a "palatal obturator" is; suffice it to say

I hated wearing them. And anyway, speaking from the pulpit I found it came naturally to put my hypernasal resonances to use; they were an oratory device, enchanting the room, all my *d*'s and *b*'s and *g*'s as I spoke would be fluted up, up through the furrow that split my very brainpan, and from where I stood in my pulpit, in the high acoustics of the chapel's lofty groins, I would hear my own nasal whistle, its reedy ringing, returning to me from lingering in the upper reaches. It cast a spell. And they loved me. I was God's clown. I was God's kicked-in-the-face adorer, my tones reverberating in the sanctuary's tallest stone sinuses. The prophet Isaiah. He was my kindred spirit, for he'd felt his own mouth to be too unclean to utter the prophecies of the Lord, until an angel touched a hot coal to his lips, which consecrated them for prophecy. Later, too, when I got in with Coldwell Banker, the crushed lip was my hood ornament. And my business card. Then at last after all the surgeries were over, I looked in the mirror at the plain ordinary lip, and I was looking through thick aquarium glass at the world. The whole world was suddenly a motel. Where I'd awoken one morning. I actually wanted to get back the way I'd been originally minted. I still do. Or rather, a small, important part of me always will.

"Well, Margot has a new lease on life, doesn't she," I said. "Thanks to the scandal of Dr. Auctor, she's got something to occupy her mind."

"She's BDD," said Thalia dismissively, speaking Group lingo. Body dysmorphic disorder: an irrational, insatiable dissatisfaction with personal appearance. BDD personality types, in their perpetual self-revision, make great return customers for cosmetic surgeons.

"You know that pre-op picture of herself?" she said. "That's not pre-op. That's from two or three operations ago. *Whoa*," she said then, because a speed bump in the Civic Center parking lot tossed the whole van. None of the developmentally disabled adults were upset. They rode on stoically. This was all routine to them. For years they'd been hitting that speed bump, at least once a week. "In fact, Margot's fine," Thalia said. "As fine as she'll ever be," she added. "We went to the Ferry Building for the market. There was a guy at the oyster bar. But she was totally blind to him. He was a sweetie and he kept *trying*. But no. She's wearing blinders where men are concerned, like a romance could send her right back in the direction of the— what is it—the Ambien bottle."

Suicide, love, lovelessness, ugliness. And power and marriage. It's amazing, how people live on the surface. I could return anytime to my Episcopal seminary mysticism, the world all around flares up in my eyes so implausibly. We have no idea what we're saying, what we're doing, any minute of the day. Nor even the thing we call a "day." What the causes. Nor what consequence. If I live to be a hundred, I'll never be able to identify fully what Thalia Kunst and I (called at birth John Gegenuber) are really saying to each other, what promises and petitions are being conveyed, too dire for us to know of. In such a way everything is sacramental, meaning never to be seen straight on, or comprehended, or quite revealed.

We had come to the far end of the parking lot. An asphalt lane led further, behind a small stucco booth, where clearly garden implements would be stored. All around were the lush park grounds of the Civic Center, Babylonian looking, artificial lagoons and willows and poplars. When Thalia squeezed the great van to a halt, behind the storage shed, the first client to get out the side door was Francesca, the pretty one with Down syndrome, the one who was about to give birth. Without taking a step further, she immediately lay down on the grass in the shade of the stucco shed.

"She's doing it again!" complained Oscar in the farthest-back seat, to Miss Kunst.

Miss Kunst paid him no attention but spoke, against the windshield, to everybody back there, "You guys know what to do."

"Miss Kunst, Francesca is going to lay there again all day."

"What would you like to do, John? It's too soon to eat, isn't it?"

"I would be happy if you gave me a rake."

"Sandy won't be long. We'll leave our food in here, and we can have a picnic later by ourselves somewhere on the way up if we want."

"She's lazy." Oscar was standing above Francesca, pointing down at her where she lay on her grassy hummock. Nobody but Oscar seemed to have any strong feelings about Francesca's wanting to lie down, as tolerance was the general rule in the group, or just an indifference in their separate zones.

"You guys take care of your own jobs and don't worry about other people's." Thalia had a key, on a stretchy little phone-cord keychain, and she was using it to open up the garden shed.

Meanwhile George, the eternally hungry one on tiptoes, had started pestering Raggedy Ann about something. I could see they were haggling. He was paying her for one of the granola bars in her possession—or promising to pay, or negotiating payment—because they were both pondering the bit of money in his open palm, while she withheld a granola bar, pressing it against her throat.

"This is the usual thing," Thalia explained, with a little pride. "Susan always manages this cornering-the-market trick."

During the ride, without our overhearing, Susan had paid a dollar—or rather promised to pay a dollar eventually—to most of the others. She was going to own all six granola bars from everybody's bag lunches. (One out of the total seven had already been eaten, by George). She didn't plan to consume any of her wealth herself. She disliked granola bars. Her only motive was to hoard them, and keep them out of George's hands, because George would have eaten all of them right away. She might sell her granola bars back to the other clients later in the day, but if she did, it would be at some higher price. In the case of the clients who were not allowed to carry pocket money, Susan would remember their debt.

Thalia was proud of Susan's clever skullduggery, but in her role, she was obliged to take control, and she made the capitalist dig into her lunch bag and return all the granola bars and forgive all her debtors. "Tomorrow," she decreed, "I keep the lunch bags and distribute them."

Tim—the alert one, the one I suspected of an arrogance— had moved up to sit in the open car doorway in the front passenger seat, the place where I'd been riding. Now, weary of the quarrel over granola bars, he heaved himself off the seat onto his feet and went into the open shed. Passing by me, he said, "A day with the tards." This was going to be his way of earning my respect, showing contempt for others. In the shed he found a rake for himself, and he told me as he went off, "If you look busy, they won't put their saliva on you." He walked out in the open to begin leaning on his rake, at a distance from the group.

The two of us who were paying attention to Tim were me and Tony, who stood beside me, the handsome one with the great leather jacket. Then Tony caught my eye, and his eyelids sank in a most lascivious way with a flick toward the Down-syndrome girl in her odalisque pose. They were all bidding to be my friend now, each in his own way. And Tony, for his part, was conveying that he'd taken sexual power over the pretty young woman who lay below him in an indolence that made her his trophy, his pelt. I was starting to see I'd entered into a complicated little family group among these seven, and by my entry I would disturb its kinship structure. Tomorrow we would all have to work together, after my sojourn with their Miss Kunst, our initiatory sojourn into the wine country and back. So our little family dynamic was only just beginning to reorder itself.

THALIA'S FRIEND SANDY, driving an identical Green Thumbs van, did appear soon. So we were free to play in the wine country. We would only have to drive back to the Green Thumbs office in our van and swap it for my big fat sedan.

However, now we would have to face the actual hedonistic dalliance—the hotel room, its bed—and I began to see I'd been harboring a half-formed contingency plan, for possible use in canceling the whole trip. It involved the telephone. I could *fake* a cell phone conversation—with Edna Goodkind or with Brandi, or with my own office—wherein I would learn that I was needed back in Marin, urgently, in person. Something like an imminent filing deadline. This was in case of certain anatomical revelations between Thalia and me that would lead only to shame and futility—certain defects, statistically possible, that we could never have the words to discuss but could share only by exposure, because they might be unimaginable as well as indescribable and, in the end, demand impossible embraces or frottage or finally the need of intervention by fertility clinicians in white coats. In my case, the particular enormity is unfixable, and my most rational fear naturally was that, unless by chance she was possessed of an enormity roughly compatible, we might discover reasons why this weekend would be barren and wretched. So this plan had taken shape in my mind. At a certain point if I saw disaster coming, I could pretend to call the office in Marin, hitting seven digits on the phone, but on the seventh digit I could press END, and then proceed to stage an imaginary conversation. Which would result in my learning I had to go home right away. It was a plan I was able to devise unsentimentally, to be deployed only if obvious need came up.

Both Green Thumbs vans bear the motto MAKIN' THINGS GROW! in letters of leprechaun green, and here came the other one, pulling around the drive of the Civic Center. Thalia's coworker Sandy during the exchange of vehicles mostly kept her eyes busy elsewhere, as if she were in on the nice little secret, that this was her friend's shot at romance. Competent, colorless, small, blonde, wearing wire-rimmed glasses, never married, a hard nub worn featureless by her dedication to these demanding big children, indeed ageless looking, she might have been thirteen. This Sandy is an instance of a certain kind of working saint I've come to know, as I recognized such sexlessness and dedication from my years in the Sausalito parish. These kinds of women infest sacristy and vestry, parlor and office. Their lives are truly and blessedly empty of passion (of course, I, with my prurient, sharp, undressing eye, I've sought deep in these church gals), seeming to be empty of desire or pleasure or even any daydream (really; I've searched) and so totally available for duty to humanity and, usually also, the quest for political power in their neighborhoods. These women are all about rulership, but over a certain limited square-footage, linoleum or carpet. I used to worry somewhat about their husbands' souls, for they're invariably married, and they're bossy, though they were never bossy with me, the beloved rector. In such ways, we all get along, in human society all interlocking, one person's weak spots plugged by another's aggressions; we would all look "developmentally disabled" if observed from above, from a cloud, we little monsters below, we little broken toys spilling about on our dark landscape, capering and scheming and seducing and outraging. Me with my priapism and my laser eye for a taint in woman—which probably was never there, not ever, except in oddball cases—it's a good thing I'm out of the pulpit. Lust, gluttony, and envy are the accomplishments I lay claim to, during my worldly slot of light, as if those were all charming attainments. But Pride is my drug of choice, Pride too far advanced to stand back and fully see. I declare my limits. In my forties now I've declared myself unwilling to "absolve, bless, and consecrate" anymore, at least publicly. Those are the powers conferred by ordination, "the ABC" as we used to call it in seminary, the little tricks I gave up practicing, as they'd begun to feel like mummery in public on my chancel elevated one step above the nave floor. But still in private, and in secret, in these years in my disguise ungowned I go around absolving and blessing and consecrating compulsively, constantly, whether watching television news or in freeway traffic or standing in a grocery checkout line, always ABC-ing: I derive a certain quiet egotistical fizz, ABC-ing everywhere, at all times and in all places but sneakily. It's the *public* and *effectual* absolve-bless-consecrate business I'm too good for. Too "intelligent" for. I make out that it's a form of humility, my unworthiness, but we all know the refinements of superiority. The implication is, well, maybe *somebody* somewhere has got to perform the antic rites, but it won't be me; I'm unfortunately just too smart. As far as I can see into myself, none of this is a deceit, or an imposture. It's as close as I've come to the truth about my life and my limits. I can have mixed pretensions about it, but it seems to be the truth.

One thing I have to show for my intellectual liberation in these bright autumn days is a BMW 750is with latte leather seats (in showroom-brochure parlance) and an exterior of "Arctic White." For Thalia's sake, I apologized for it, in my usual way, giving her my line about how it's a necessity of the realtor's trade, while I stowed her suitcase in the trunk. She had gone inside the Green Thumbs offices and changed into a different outfit—a simple white scoop-neck shirt, and a pair of those faded jeans women spend a hundred dollars for, which, on her, outlined that hip so glamorous, so athletic, so packed, a torsion bar. This was my girlfriend. I had a girlfriend. There she was. Not only was she a girlfriend, but she was Thalia! Stowing a suitcase in a car's trunk felt like an act distinctly hymeneal. But I told myself this wasn't really an illicit outing. It was a perfectly legitimate (if hymeneal, Lord) trip to a wine-country spa, people do this all the time, every day on the freeway you pass people who are doing something like this. My doctrinaire misgivings about extramarital sex are an affectation I can throw away instantly, throwing away thirty years of convictions, in sweet rescue by hypocrisy, as I lowered the lid of my trunk upon Thalia's supple leather suitcase. It lay in there now beside my own more masculine practical thing of heavy black armored square fabric with reinforced Kevlar corners. Thalia got her own car door, and as I came around, she had already—in her infinite generosity—begun talking, opening the fountain of easy conversation that would forfend awkwardness, throughout this whole two-day ordeal. If it were me setting the tone, the weekend would be all long embarrassed silences. She was talking about her seven clients—the seven dwarves, as she and Sandy and the other staff liked to call them. They assign them roles like Sleepy, Sneezy, Grumpy, Dopey—but also they innovate on the seven dwarves' traditional names with tags like Horny, Pissy, Greedy—and she was describing how excited everyone was about Francesca's baby.

"We're a family. They're the siblings, I'm the mom. You'll see. You'll get to be the dad tomorrow when we go up to Dr. Auctor's estate to cut the grass." Her thinking, here, was pleasingly similar to my own. "So for them, it's like, they're getting a new baby brother when Francesca comes due. That's how it feels to them. Except Tim. He sees himself in the role of dad, I think. He always wants to gang up with me against the others, and be the husband. So we even have an Oedipal thing going on in our little family. He likes to police George, keep him from putting his glue on the girls." (George has an old mucilage bottle he's attached to, which Thalia had told me about. The mucilage inside is dried up, but he loves the old stabbing applicator nozzle, of soft red rubber with a slit tip, and he chases the girls with it, pretending to apply stickiness.)

Facing the weekend squarely, I swung the car out onto Fifth toward the freeway entrance ramp. It comes up right away after a block or so, and I took that familiar left turn I'd taken an infinite number of times as a realtor all over the county, and before that as a minister, on many kinds of errands; life goes by so fast.

I was leaving my own world in a mess. The dashboard clock read 1:30, and it was really time to call Edna Goodkind's house. Edna would be at home sitting at her cluttered kitchen table, amid her small village of amber prescription bottles and paper napkins and well-studied mail-order catalogues (I knew that kitchen table well), stale cookies arranged on a plate. Brandi McCannon by now had been at Edna's for some while, at that kitchen table, most convivially distracting Edna, while the inspector worked. I knew I ought to pull off the freeway and call. I had a feeling the secret motives for this second inspection would be revealed tomorrow: Brandi would call in the morning, Sunday, with a new offer maybe. But I really had to face this before leaving Marin, so I patted my cell phone in my pocket to make sure it was there, and I turned on my blinker to get off at the next exit.

THALIA SAID SHE understood. Go ahead and call. So I got off where a frontage road dead-ends at marshy land, and I went out to stand on the roadside and dial.

"John!" said Brandi's voice. "Here we are! It's a party here. Edna got out some snacks."

"Hi, Brandi. May I talk to Edna? You know, all I really want to do is check on her. Make sure she feels all right with this little invasion. You know, she's ninety-one."

"Oh, it couldn't be further from that. We're having a blast. But I'll get her. I'm sure she'd like to talk to you."

It took a while for Edna to make the journey to the phone. Inside the car, Thalia poked at the radio dial. When Edna did come on the line, there was a lot of clanking and rustling, and then she said, "John? Is that you?"

I could tell right away today was one of the days when Edna's metabolism was on the slow side. She has some good days and some not-so-good days, when her comprehension of events around her isn't great, and she seems almost to be mourning again the death of her husband.

"It's me," I said. "How are things going? Is the inspector there?"

"He's very painstaking."

"Good. Well, that's their job."

"John, is he going to lay carpets?"

"Carpets? No, Edna. He's the house inspector. He's exactly like the house inspector who came before. Remember the other house inspector? He's looking the house over, to make sure everything's shipshape. Before selling it. You know, we're going to sell your house, remember."

She sighed, "Yes, that's right, we're going to sell it to those two nice children. I thought it was carpeting, because he has a roller gadget. It's on the end of a stick and he's measuring things."

"That's right, he has to measure things sometimes. It's called a DigiRoller, and maybe he's measuring distances to electrical outlets. Did you get out your cookies? I'm sure Brandi and her contractor friend would love to eat some of those cookies."

"Well, John? Did you know about the crack in the foundation?"

There is no crack in Edna's foundation, none to speak of, and this was a fulfillment of my worst suspicions. I wouldn't have expected Brandi to resort to this, because what's the motive? She doesn't want a *lower* price on the house. She seems to want to queer the whole deal, in some way.

"A crack? No, you'll have to show me, Edna. I'll come over there Monday morning and we'll have a look. You know a little hairline crack isn't going to undermine anything."

"And there's powder-post beetles. Did you know about them?"

"I'll get a copy of the report—the inspection report—and we'll go through it line by line."

"It's a terrible name, 'powder-post'! Just picture that. Omar was also an entomologist, too, but I've never heard of anything like that! Powder-post! Isn't that just an awful thing?"

"I want to check into all of this for you Monday, Edna. Can I talk to Brandi? Is she there?"

When Brandi came to the phone, I said, "Brandi, five-seventy is a fair price for this house."

Brandi made a tragic sigh of universal sympathy. "I didn't put a crack in the foundation, John." She was making was a soteriological point: *God* put the crack in the foundation, and since I'd been a minister, I could be a big boy about that. "But let's discuss this later today. I'll get back to the castle and I'll call you. We can discuss this. I promise you."

The *I promise you* was code: its ulterior meaning was to advertise to me a rational agreement she wanted to enter into. Something we might discuss over Edna's head, and outside her hearing.

"Who is this inspector?"

"Hey, did you know the origin of the word *mollusk*? We've been having a party, and Edna is a blast. The word *mollusk* comes from the Greek word *mollusca*, which just means *icky*." By the grin in her tone, she was sharing a gaze with Edna as she spoke. They were girls who'd gotten into the cookie jar together. Maybe they'd taken down some of her sherry. "Anything icky, that's a mollusk, and mollusks lead absolutely depraved lives."

"I guess I'll talk with you Monday. Can it wait till Monday? I'm going to be out of town all weekend."

"Oh? You are?"

She would have liked asking where I would be. Brandi is always collecting espionage, and my weekend's absence was interesting. "I'll call you Monday, Brandi." Edna Goodkind's rescue could wait till Monday.

OUR ROOM WAS beautiful of course, overlooking a fairway. We didn't golf. Thalia really doesn't care about golf, though she gamely pretended she had always wanted to try. I think she wouldn't have the patience for it. In golf's ambling spacious world of—interspersed—silences and garrulity, Thalia's body type and soul wouldn't collaborate. I certainly didn't want to be golfing myself, either. I've done my share of it, during my cunning days as a minister. Even as a "fisher of men," I've gone out on the links with many an old geezer, all too often angling for money in some indirect way, as winning souls often hangs on money. It may not be a surprising revelation—that a minister in his parish is a wily scamming entrepreneur, even if he disguise it under lubricant unction, and even toss out a well-timed dirty joke in the right crowd. I miss that, how invigorating it is, practicing avarice so *successfully* in sheep's clothing. More than the sentimental memories one might imagine, more than the incense smell or the wonderful old music or the ostensible joys of charity (because the paradox of charity is, when you see a lot of it close up, it's pretty murky, both in its motives and in its ends, and even stinks), I miss what a good manipulator I was. What a politician. I mourn the creative license. An ecclesiastic is licensed to sneak up on folks in a way that a realtor is disqualified from.

There wasn't much left of the afternoon. So after a couple of visits to the near wineries (which neither of us cared about, or really *saw*, or were even conscious of as we strolled), and eschewing golf, we came inside and had them send up dinner on a cart and didn't go out at all, but just stayed in, beautiful though we were. In our so-called suite, we ended up—without planning on this—sitting chastely side by side on a small couch watching television. We maintained, I would estimate, about twenty to twenty-four inches of space between us.

We were avoiding the area of the bed. Our "suite" was divided with half partitions into separate spaces, so we didn't always have to lay eyes on the bed, even with peripheral vision. There was just the one bed. It was the room Thalia had reserved. As we sat there, she and I both knew—all bifurcatives know this, all the cleft and cloven will know (that strange English verb *cleave*, in all its conjugations signifying both a halving and a clinging), all the rabbit-mouthed and the riven, even sitting side by side on a couch, all will be familiar with the embryological origin of their disfigurement: that in our mothers' wombs at some time in about the twelfth day of gestation when we were still germs on a uterine wall, there came a point, a point when our little normal clump of cells was slightly more complicated than, say, a tube but less complicated than a whistle. At that time, there came one little moment when the wad of cells didn't exactly differentiate on symmetrical lines. There was a bleb. So as mature creatures walking the earth we may remain open along the whole meridian, from vomer through septum and philtrum to perineum, a fontanel unclosed, a scimitar slash opening privacy to the fluting of the public. We'll never lose this vulnerability. Thalia and I stayed glued to the television screen, cemented there. The programming was distracting and loud, even enjoyable; prime-time television is such a sugary drink for the gaze. The show was a popular talent competition, in which beautiful young people were singing and trying, by outshining their competition, to become American pop idols. That was the conceit of the show: the instant apotheosis of ordinary kids from obscurity. They were competing to win the love of the television audience, who voted immediately by calling an 800 number. It was sad, watching them hope and try. Swinging their hips, putting a sparkle in their eyes. The vocal style that predominates, nowadays, is a dazzling sketch-around-the-note style, derived from the real grandeur of the Negro gospel, where the voice improvises in loops and figure eights all around the pitch. Nobody hits the notes straight-on anymore; they warble decoratively in the vicinity of the notes. One beautiful white girl, sounding as black as she could, was belting out her climax, poking all around the true, ultimate note. And Thalia beside me scared me a little by making a risky joke. In her tone of bleakest sympathy, she said of the singer, "She's looking for the G-spot."

It goes without saying that, as grown-ups in modern society, we are aware of such a coarse construction of love. We all see the magazine covers at the supermarket checkout stand. But to admit to the awareness, to be so casual and flippant about it, will perhaps be one of the generational differences between Thalia and me. Admittedly it was a funny remark, watching the singer's look of anxious doubt while her voice groped.

"Looking for the *song's* G-spot," I said. Or rather *explained*—because it seems I can't resist the temptation to flatten wit, to literalize, rationalize, overexplain, deflate. Francis Bacon wrote, "Reading maketh an exact man, conversation maketh a ready man." And I suppose, if I'm deficient in "readiness," it's only because I haven't had enough practice at this. Earlier that same day, standing in the bright sunlight in the alley behind Green Thumbs, my gratitude for Thalia's denim overalls was truly pious and cowardly; beneath the bib panel the easy-to-picture, standard dual mammary swells, of a kind to be viewed on fckm.com or baadboy.com, ducts for lactation, the planes of torso and hip, inguinal fold, gluteal sulcus, the female flare of hip and, at the nadir, beneath the OshKosh denim, the unseeable gill breathing atmospheres metaphysical and futuristic and eschatological: all this is protected from me, and I from it, by the intervention of denim, and *she* from it, too.

"Looking for all of America's G-spot," she added. (The title of the television series is *American Idol.* It names the thing they're all competing to be.)

She sipped her wine.

This was how I'd always imagined marriage. I could get used to it. An unembarrassment. An unworriedness. An eccentricity. Thalia hadn't wanted to go out—to a movie or a fancy restaurant where we could take our beautiful new faces out for a spin. She wanted to stay in. I never watch commercial programming, though I do have a TV—and blessed Thalia, she doesn't even own one!—but I could see that, if we were married, we might watch TV. We could watch shallow unredeeming TV, because we'd both be there.

"We had a funny crisis at Green Thumbs this morning," she went on, tilting her glass at the singer, because this was somehow pertinent. "Our two snails got stuck together, like face-to-face, and we couldn't unstick them. We have two pet snails. In a bowl together. The whole class named them Jason and Scar. That's their names." She cast me one arch glance. "Jason and Scar are supposed to stick on the glass and walk around, of course. But somehow these two found each other. Everything came to a halt. All the gang was in a panic." (I wasn't sure how this pertained. Unless it had to do with a singer unable to come unstuck from her note. It was just another Thalia-sequitur enriching my life.) "Like, if somebody was *suffocating,* the panic couldn't have been worse. In the end I had to reach in and separate Jason and Scar, very delicately, with utmost delicacy."

All these Thalia-sequiturs I would treasure as poetical, if/when we were married. It was possible that, sitting on that couch with our gazes trained parallel forward, we could both feel ourselves sinking into a familiar connect-the-dots way of talking. Her mind (I first saw this way back in Recovery Group) makes swerves that I alone will know how to cherish and curate.

"Why don't you get your own inspection?" she said. Alarm went through me. She added, "Of Edna's house."

"Oh," I said, and took a breath and sipped my own wine. "Once an inspector slams a house, it stays slammed. A made-up foundation crack is as bad as any real foundation crack. It's a rumor. It sticks. But I think she's got some other thing up her sleeve. Brandi, I mean. I just have to wait till Monday to see what she develops with this."

On television, we watched the gay contestant taking his seat at the piano, his mascara, his starry eyes, his unfortunate prominent jaw. A little bone reduction wouldn't be expensive for him, especially for a young, talented, charismatic person whose personal beauty might be part of the profession he aspires to. I knew from Group that he could get that jaw reduced for about ten or twelve thousand dollars.

"It's all baloney anyway," said Thalia, by way of consolation. "Every house has a crack in the foundation. Since the beginning of time, you can always find a crack. Those people will buy the house with or without."

I was surprised. She was so right: buying a house is a matter of the heart, and she could *see* the whole real estate profession is mostly just a shamanistic, magical business of standing to one side.

I said, "'Scar'?" The name of the schoolhouse snail.

She replied, "'Scarlett.'" This in a deadpan fatigue I liked.

"Mm-hm," I said.

So at that point, recognizing what was inevitable, she said lightly, "I'm sleepy. Let's do the hot tub."

We agreed we could take turns using the bathroom, to change into our suits.

TO SIT IN a hot tub is a hellish kind of pastime. And an unhealthy one. There are serious health concerns. It raises the body temperature above normal and causes such blood-vessel dilation, people risk passing out and losing consciousness. Every ten minutes or so, if you feel faint, you need heave up and sit on the rim and expose your poached flesh not only to the grip of cold night air but also to the inspection of your friends. We "turned on the bubbles" because, in the cylinder of water like a Lucite paperweight, our thighs and everything came up into sharp pale focus. Better to hide ourselves in the circle of surf and speak disembodied above its roar. Thalia's and my respective morphological peculiarities, where they were wadded down in their pinches, *they* were always lying in wait, all weekend lodged deep. The whole day had been a shrinking arena. Now just a cauldron. Whenever one of us sat up on the rim of the tub to cool off, the other made a perfect show of not letting his eyes be attracted. In my case, I had the loose boxer style of swim trunks. For Thalia, women's technologies of concealment and revelation provide a design of—in this case, tonight—a bathing suit with a skirtlike panel, to accomplish a similar sleight. At least it released my eyes from an obligation to glance. Finally, at one point we were talking about various scar-tissue-healing ointments we'd used, or heard about, when she said something—at last!—that allowed me to sur-mise—and with what a bump of unexpected joy—that she was indeed deformed. Do I have any right? To rejoice? She'd been plugging a kind of commercial poultice tape she and Margot both have been using. "The package says 'Neosporin,' but it doesn't have an antibiotic, it's just the same manufacturers as Neosporin. It's in any drug store."

Sitting below her, I had been praising the perfection of her new mouth. And as she basked in that, she kept offering me a quarter-profile view, daubing cheek and philtrum with a sculpting finger, where her Neosporin product had melted away any thread of pewter in the flesh she might have imagined. "Margot gets all the latest techniques and drugs because, as I say, she's over-the-top."

I said in a sigh of involuntary awe (she was sitting elevated on the rim), "It certainly does seem to work with you."

"You're supposed to sleep with it on. But the sticky stuff wears out, and they fall off. You have to use a Band-Aid or something. I'm using Scotch tape."

"I think I'll just keep on with the old Mederma cream. I'm probably about as healed as I'm going to get anyway."

At that point, after a pause, she admitted, with a whine of beseeching higher powers, "I just don't *want* any more surgery."

There it was. The hint. It was all in her tone: the dread and chagrin. My jubilation was not immediate but rather grew gradually inside, over the subsequent minutes of conversation as I licensed happiness in small climbing increments: the joy inside was like a twisted cloth that, when twisted to an overtight rope, eventually pops up, from a rope to a hard, climbing knot. There was that knot. She and I were two people whose only kiss, last week in her apartment doorway, had been as strange and ritual as setting two apples in contact. She had leaned against her door-post, and almost diplomatically we put our closed mouths in tan-gency. That was all. We were both aware that we were testing new faces, and the awkwardness for both of us had a certain detached humor—that's how we were getting through it. We were almost bringing faint smiles together, not open mouths. But then, as we embraced in her apartment doorway, the inevitable was making itself felt in remote or at least unmapped dimensions. This morning on the phone, when she broke in on herself, pleading, "John, I want to do the winery tour," her voice was referring back to that moment, standing in her doorway, the nether motion. When she said it, we both knew. The structure of chronological time is spongiform with time-travel tunnels: her winery-tour appeal tunneled directly back, through five days, to the shift of a hip in a doorway. Precisely that was in her tone of voice.

But later that night after we had once consummated the inevitable, in the bed that was within short staggering distance of the hot tub, and while we lay there afterward under the sheets, Thalia found herself cornered into revealing the new source of a much more terrible awkwardness, something she had been keeping to herself, in order not to frighten me away, a secret that was living inside her as painfully as a congenital malformation. Or more painfully. For a defect in the body is an easy affliction compared to a defect in the soul.

We had decided to be silly and order Champagne from room service, because a pair of secretly deformed people who have at last found each other do have something to celebrate. Thalia has a wonderful sense of how the formal and the ridiculous can combine. Thus the Champagne. And after I'd hung up the phone upon the forbearing night concierge, she said, "John, there's something about myself. I ought to tell you this. It's something interesting."

I was as revved up as an adolescent, or I could have been; if I were an emotionally reckless type, I might have swung on a chandelier. Nothing she could confess would dim the moral triumph, the spiritual triumph, the practical triumph. I'm not going to say anything further to describe, O prurient reader, the congress of two congenitally unique aberrant individuals. I, myself, as a scholar of the new variations of porn, and as a moviegoer, am aware of course that the contemporary version of copulation is very highly dramatized, a thrashing, like alligators, alligators in combat rather than coitus. Nevertheless, sex, still, does make idiots of us. Again, the ridiculous and the formal combine. Particularly an idiot of the male. In a way it's the male's most gallant role, his idiocy. No amount of the best-intentioned feminism will change the fact that women love a baseness in man. Thalia and I were both reluctant and considerate but also surprised by what form delight takes; the word *surprise* sums up the sensation, how it isn't exactly pleasure but more like necessity, once the current gets a grip and you're moving downstream fast. On a strictly mental level, there was a certain amount of relief and satisfaction that, after all these years, there was nothing to forbid this, a calculation soon smothered deep in the general spilling out at the end of the long slope. Then in the aftermath in that point at which we were most matrimonially glued together, particularly in the case of two structurally unique people who have found each other, Thalia had this deeper secret to reveal to me. It was a fact about herself which, she worried, might now cause me to fear her, and maybe actually want to ditch her, even after this.

First, I ought to explain something about myself. I think I've always been attracted to a little oddness in women, or even, to speak frankly, an open "craziness" in women. At least it's how things tend to turn out.

What do I mean by that? Over the years, I've noticed that a woman who excites my notice, or even my obsession, will show herself early on to have a certain corrupt sparkle, a scent of the unpredictable, even of disaster. Many men, I suppose, want merely a dependable helpmate (that is, if a fellow has been able to be rational and overcome the blinding barrier of beauty, and to see a little deeper in, which even for the wisest doesn't necessarily always happen). If I were like a lot of men, maybe I'd want someone with, simply, a personality in tasteful creams and vanillas, as to harmonize with my BMW interior, someone kosher who will support the continuity of life. But I find that I, peculiarly, ask also that a woman bring a little fresh, sharp wind into my world.

I seem to be referring to the various "loves of my life." Don't think a minister hasn't had plenty of actual problems with romance. Even a cleft-palate minister. Even a virgin. My particular harelip was never, as you may picture, the drastic gash in the vermillion. The result of a childhood corrective operation by an inexperienced surgeon, bought at a bargain by my unsophisticated parents: it's always had more the crushed look of a lip pressed to a wineglass. The more repulsive problem was my speaking voice, clarinet reed in my nose. Yet the truth is, even a marred, snerfling, celibate, bookish minister can be beloved, beloved by even beautiful and brilliant women, *especially* the beauties and the smart ones, given the dreary experiences certain "beautiful" women will have had with the sort of men they attract; it's a risk to a fortunately formed woman, that society can so paint her with lotions she becomes sealed inside her person, grabbable by the wrong kind of man, and then eventually herself hardhearted. So ended many a Sausalito marriage. Thus, I think, a homely minister can look safe. And courtly love, where touch is forbidden, can cause dizzying eroticism, take my word. I would say I've perhaps been a greater rake and a seducer than a lot of men who actually do copulate—as if that were the only trophy they got, the carcass itself. For a number of men do get the carcass while staying completely oblivious of who exactly it was. (Fortunately, there are women for such men, women who don't want to be found out, and have agendas of their own, sometimes not-very-providential agendas.)

Anyway, in my secret passages as a lover and a beloved, in sacristy or in rectory office, I've noticed that many of my passions mostly involve an unpredictable woman, a perverse woman, a peculiar one. A sense of humor is terrifically important, and humor seems to involve rule-breaking, mischief, transgression. It isn't funny if it doesn't risk something. In this way, at least in my world, the woman that sets fire to a room is the more attractive. And she can be a headache. The kind who has loved me is the kind who may phone at three in the morning with an odd notion; or drink too much and secretly suck on cigarettes in a basement; or plant worries in my mind for no purpose except to see me worry; or fly off on tangents that make *everybody* worry. It's mostly married ones I did my profoundest flirting with, as a minister. Their suburban husbands tend to be faithful, persecuted, invariably handsome galoots, for whom I have sympathy. Sometimes I think maybe they were the brutal kind who got the carcass only, but often my cuckolds will have been simply handsome, oblivious, not-too-smart innocents. This flirting of mine (at Christmas parties or at some country club, in cloakroom and vestry, in the rectory or on retreats), while it has never been consummated, has been spiritually consummated, quite intoxicatingly and multiply consummated, at moments of truth and intimacy, so that I've known these women as their husbands never could. We've slain each other, these women and I.

In the costume of a real estate agent these days, as I say, I'm not so appealing. Maybe one assumes a "real estate agent" is on the make in general. And one's guard goes up. The ministry was my glory day, as a sex object. Nevertheless, though I may not any longer have such a chance with them, the women I continue to notice and desire are the eccentrics, the ones with the mad sparkle, and I have to admit, Thalia was consistent with the pattern. From the first visible restlessness of her hip, when she sat in the circle of Recovery Group folding chairs, and from the tempo of an idle pencil tapping in her fingers; from the first uncalled-for birdlike tilt of the head, as if some phantom earphone were feeding her rather alarming commentary; her gummi-worm jewelry; her guilty giggle; her poking a finger in an ear and screwing it around; and then the reward of my hopes for wit when she joked, in Group, that Margot Maitland in all her cosmetic surgeries was "nibbling her way on up to amputations"—in every sign, Thalia has shown an ability to zigzag seizing on truth. It's a brilliance that I stand aside from, and love helplessly as revelation.

But then when she and I were sitting up in the bedsheets waiting for the Champagne to arrive, the sparkle took on an aspect of contagion, because what she said was, "I ought to tell you, I'm not really myself."

She was so intense about this her eyes appeared slightly crossed, looking straight at me.

"I haven't been myself since 2002. I can tell you the exact day. It was March 25, 2002, at two thirty in the afternoon."

"Oh?" I said.

"The day I stopped being myself. The person you now see before you turned up in Boise, in the airport. I was supposed to fly in and visit my grandmother. But I swear I walked out of that plane at the terminal gate and I could not remember what I was doing. Or why I was there. Or who I was. I went down to the rent-a-car place and I rented a car—like with a credit card, driver's license, student ID card—it all said 'Thalia Kunst'—and all this time I'm hoping at some point I could figure out who I was and where I was going. But I never did. I had an ID. My ID said I was somebody. And I had the car reservation. But I was suddenly so stupid, and I was thinking maybe I could just get out of the airport and drive to wherever—like to the address on my driver's license or something. Even though that wasn't Idaho. I mean, I knew I was in Idaho. I knew I was 'Thalia Kunst.' I knew that much. It's weird, I knew some things, but I totally lost certain other things. This was a strictly neurological phenomenon. It's got a diagnosis and everything. I started driving—just hoping!—like hoping!—and by the end of that day, I was in this little town in the far north end of Idaho in this roadside sporting-goods store—standing in the racks of all these shirts and spandex stuff and Patagonia stuff, crying, and despairing. Because I'd lost myself. Stanley, Idaho. That was the name of the town. That's where I started my new life. It's a condition called fugue. It's called dissociative fugue. It's like: you know how you can go in your pantry and look in the cupboard but you forgot what you were looking for? It's like that, but it's everything. And it goes on. Some dissociative-fugue people do remember. Some never do. I never did. It's kinda like schizophrenia but different. That is"— she set a hand on my arm—"it's not schizophrenia. It's nothing to do with clinical schizophrenia. It's just really weird."

"You were how old?"

"Nineteen. Nineteen, in with all those racks of spandex bicycle outfits. With no idea who I was."

"So it's like amnesia."

"Well, yes, but it's fugue. Amnesia is the symptom, but dissociative fugue is the diagnosis."

"Well, Thalia! My God! Didn't your family come looking for you?"

"Oh, yeah, yes, of course. A hospital in Boise helped, and I got back home. But from then on, my mom and dad were a pair of very nice strangers. I started from blank. I never did get anything back, of my previous life. They looked for possible brain tumors and such. But there was nothing. I was nineteen, and I was *told* I'd been a psychology major, so I did continue with psychology. I mean, I could look at my transcript. There it was. It showed the courses I'd taken. And what the hell, all the clothes in the closet fit me."

"Thalia!" I said again. Just to speak the name *Thalia* wasn't sufficient: it was like pinning a paper cut-out dress on her—or like embracing her—nothing would exactly suffice.

"In my college courses, I had to fill in some lost practical information. I seemed to know certain things, like where classes were. And what my teachers' names were. My friends looked familiar, but I didn't remember *their* names. But I remembered the course material. That was a paradox. I did well on all the exams."

"How do you get along with your family today?"

"Fine. Fine. We're fine. My mom's still alive. But now, the fact remains, I never did have a long history with them. We have a history only since I was twenty. I'm like this visitor, at least in my own mind. To them I stayed, still, very much their daughter. They remember me from the beginning. I'm their same old troublesome daughter. But, John?" Her hand lifted from my arm. It went back to her own lap, as if touch were now not such a good idea. "It has happened since then. It has recurred, a little bit. I was in San Diego two years ago. And I was crossing a parking lot in a mall. This time it only lasted for a half hour, then I got back to myself. But it was definitely the fugue again. I just had the feeling. It's tingly. And suddenly, I had no idea why I was in San Diego or what I was doing. You may not believe it, but it's totally, completely terrifying. I had to sit down, it was right next to the parking lot, in a little outdoor restaurant place. Like, I was crossing the parking lot and I happened to be aiming at a chair on the outside part of the restaurant, so I just kept going and sat down on that chair. It was a white wrought-iron chair, and it was at a glass-topped table, and I sat there. I still knew who I was: that was the key; I hadn't forgotten myself. I also did retain a general idea why I was in San Diego, but I couldn't have found my way back to my hotel, just then. And I had no idea why I was crossing an asphalt parking lot headed for a wrought-iron chair. It was like my whole skull made a bang and emptied out, and all I could do was head straight for the wrought-iron chair and sit down and hope no one would notice me. And hope no waiter would come up and say 'Can I do something for you.'"

She shrugged her bare shoulders above the bedclothes' upheld splash, her body here solid evidence, evidence of a personality, physically with me in bed.

Right then, the swooping, attacking violins of "Night on Bald Mountain" came up loud. The music was originating at my cell phone, on the bedside table. It was also doing its vibrating drumroll on the wood veneer as it sang.

This was past ten o'clock, on a Saturday night. The caller was going to be Brandi McCannon, I knew it, the unsleeping hundred-eyed watcher of Marin real estate, and I knew I ought to answer it. If I wanted to stay ahead of Brandi's newest strategies I ought to answer it. And I ought to answer it if I was a professional, if I was serious about going on in my career as a realtor in the county.

So I did answer it, with a show of helpless annoyance, for Thalia's benefit. In a way I was thankful for the diversion and the side pocket. The call wouldn't take long, then after I'd hung up there would be a reacquaintance with the woman I'd found at last, an acquaintance on this new basis, wherein Thalia would be astonished to find that her troubles and imperfections were welcomed with rejoicing, that her particular craziness, whatever it was, might be a country I'd always wanted to visit.

Brandi said, "Hi, John. Where are you? Are you at home?"

It was typical of her, wanting that piece of information.

"What can I do for you, Brandi?"

"I'm just closing up here, I'm at the castle, and John, I thought I ought to tell you, because it's going to mean reframing your plans. Edna Goodkind is a darling and she's going to be my client. She loves you *of course*, but she's going to switch. It's purely business, not personal. Century 21 is just in a better position to get her better offers and a fast closing."

I actually knew this was going to happen. When "Night on Bald Mountain" started playing, somehow subconsciously I was already turning to face this, the penalty for my day of much-deserved selfishness in Napa. Still, I was going to put up a show of fighting it. "That's illegal, Brandi. It's a split-commission sale—"

"No, it isn't, not since Shawn and Cheese have withdrawn their offer. And since Edna has taken it off the market."

"Edna? Has taken her house off the market?"

"Oh, John, you have to check your mail. You have to keep your mail constantly open, or on mobile. I don't know how to do business with you otherwise. If you're not in touch?"

"Brandi, I'm going to have to take this in to Mitchell Boulevard." Mitchell Boulevard is the Board of Realtors offices. They do dispute resolutions, ethics arbitrations.

"John? Listen. If I'm risking losing you as a friend, then you can have Edna back. Really, John, just calm down. Because I value you as a friend far more than I value the percentage on this five-seventy in Gerstle Park. You're my friend, John. You're the most integritied person I know in this scene! Or in my life! You're the man I trust. I can't have you feeling like I've betrayed you. You can keep Edna if you want. If you feel I've gone behind your back."

She waited for a response, but I had none. I was dizzy. Why had she called? What was her motive?

"I'm serious, John. You're the man. I'll never forget when Mindy caught you doing an exorcism on the Rick Shantih house in Kentfield."

"Oh, Jesus, that wasn't an exorcism, for Christ's sake; there's no such thing anyway. And that wasn't anything, it was just some little well-wishing thing."

Thalia was behind me leaning up against the bedstead listening to this. As the conversation became outlandish, she didn't seem to perk up or get alarmed. But my back was turned.

"John," Brandi's voice was oil-on-the-waters now, trying to calm me down. "You happen to have a spiritual groundedness which, to me, is unique in this day and age. That's all. I respect that immensely."

"Can we talk in the morning? It's past my bedtime. We spiritual types, you know, us priests and medicine men, we go to bed early."

I pressed the END button on the phone. I pressed it *while* her voice was going on (insisting we would talk again tomorrow, we could work this all out, she'd be in her office until ten, but after that, she had two showings in San Rafael, it was Sunday . . .)

I put the phone back on the table, and I leaned back against the bedstead beside Thalia, whose arms were folded. I folded my arms like hers.

"Hanky-panky in the real estate business," I explained.

"I could hear. She's got one of those voices that cuts through. She sounds formidable. Who is Shawn and Cheese? Is that a real estate firm?"

"No. Ha. Shawn and Cheese are two human beings, one male, one female. Youngsters, you might say. They want to buy a house. Or they did."

While I spoke, I decided that they did still want that house. The sale would go through. And Brandi would now get both ends of the deal. Six percent rather than three percent.

"Well, Brandi sounds . . ." she reverted, "formidable all right."

"Brandi is a very hard worker. She deserves all the success she's getting. She's probably the highest-paid agent in Marin."

For a minute in gloomy admiration of Brandi McCannon, we both sat there, arms folded. We were viewing in defeat a parade float, advertising "Brandi McCannon," that had materialized in the room at the foot of our bed.

I decided to face this other new issue head-on, and I said, "I used to be an Episcopal minister. That's *my* dark secret I've been keeping from you."

She already knew, because she gave me her crazed glare and said, "John, you've got 'minister' sticking out all over. Besides, I know all about you. I had you thoroughly investigated by my spies."

"If you've known, how come you didn't mention it? Or bring it up?"

"You're embarrassed about it. This is according to my spies. *Ambiguous* about it," she amended, misusing that word perhaps.

"So the house in question," I told her, "the house in Kentfield that Brandi mentioned, was a pretty famous house, because it was a big mansion owned by the wife of Rick Shantih."

Thalia looked at me for a minute, absorbing this, and then she said, "And the wife tried to burn the house down." She'd seen it in the papers at the time. It was all very lurid.

It was a notorious case in Marin County. Not only in Marin but all over the world, Rick Shantih is so internationally beloved an artist and musician, at least in his particular genre of New Age meditation music, that when his wife was sent to jail, she was viewed popularly as a goblin.

"Brandi McCannon and I did the sale on that house. She was the agent for a nice new family who was coming over from Iran, and I was Rick Shantih's agent. We split the commission. And frankly, before escrow closed, I thought I was all alone in the place one day, and I just *happened* to be there, and I *thought* I would indulge a little old superstition and go around banishing a few bad vibes. There were bad vibes. You know. Truly awful things had happened there. The Anglican Church, for your information, does have a little thing. It's not an 'exorcism,' with a house. With a house it's just called a 'clearance.' It's one of their quaint, antiquated old things they can't quite get out of the liturgy, and it's just a few words in the Book of Occasional Services, to just say a vague little prayer. Like, there used to be an agent at Coldwell Banker who would burn sage. That was her purifying thing. Whenever she made a sale, she would go through a house at close of escrow, carrying some smoldering sage. Even if you don't expect 'results.' Or get specifically superstitious. It's just a few words to make the place feel subjectively better."

"His wife was awful! Sue Glaspel! You wonder what somebody like Rick Shantih ever saw in her! And she had that forehead. Wasn't it like a receding hairline she had?"

"They'd been married all their lives. But it's true. Also, with her, photographs in newspapers didn't reproduce kindly. And I think it's possible that editors, in her case, *picked* those kinds of photos. Whereas of course Rick's photographs are controlled by his managers. But it's true, she probably wasn't aging well. She was always his bookkeeper. She was his business manager really. They'd been married thirty years."

"But going out and burning down his mansion?"

"It wasn't his mansion. It was hers. She was rich. She came from money, and he'd married that. Also, she didn't premeditate that crime. She threw a can of gasoline in the fireplace."

Thalia had already heard the ugly details, and like everybody, she was half in love with Rick Shantih, who was great looking, a mascot for all Marin County, whose music you couldn't hear without getting happy—and who also was famous for devoting *all* of his entertainment income to certain charitable causes, particularly agencies to adopt African babies out of jungle villages to place them with American families. That was his flagship cause. That he had a wife at all was something few people knew; it was for obvious reasons a record-industry secret, until she threw a can of gasoline in the fire and he prosecuted.

"Anyway, we helped Mr. Shantih sell that house and get his half, after the divorce. After she was in jail. So he came out all right. And I'll tell you, I just felt like this nice young couple from Iran was buying the house—plus, they had a brand-new baby girl—and I just felt like going through those rooms and just saying a few prayerlike words—because I'll tell you the truth, I don't *judge* anyone—I don't try to 'evaluate' or even reconstruct, for example, what went on in those rooms between the Glaspels—because that's a nice effect of the whole 'prayer' gadget: you refrain from judging people and being tempted to come slamming down—which is *actually* what I *really* love to do, and do so very well—but whatever happened in those rooms when Rick Glaspel lived there,"—(I always veer towards Mr. Shantih's real name rather than his apotheotic)—"I just felt like I wanted to go through and say a few little words. And then I came out in the big grand marble foyer, and there's Mindy Golden, Brandi McCannon's friend at Century 21—standing there smirking. She was the one who started calling it an exorcism."

Thalia's arms were still folded, and she was still staring out at the "Brandi McCannon" parade float—the big 3-D hologram of it—that had invaded our room. Which would be gradually fading under her gaze. Her forearms latching tight, and yet tighter, she looked deserted; she looked all alone in the existential wilderness of having lost her identity at age nineteen in Stanley, Idaho.

"Is she allowed to do that?" she asked dreamily, remotely. "Can she take your client away?"

She didn't really care about an answer. And I wanted to get off the subject of Brandi McCannon. Back to the subject of Thalia. Her more pressing, more interesting existential problem.

Squeak of a room service cart's wheel. It had been coming up the corridor. Then came a soft knock at the door and a muffled voice, "Champagne, sir. Good night, sir." I had asked that the cart be left outside and that the porter leave, so we wouldn't be disturbed.

I took advantage of the moment to make a helpful little joke, stirring around in the bedclothes, inclining to her so my whole body, farcically, was raked too far over in her direction: the intoxicating smell of her, the amazing organism beside me, female soul, corridor of light slanting upward, right there in my midst, zenith of evolution, my dawning road, extending out light years, the whole Milky Way, embryonic brine, all its luminance, and also the sore worried intellect, right there to soothe. "Anyway, dearie, I think I could still love you, even if I have to fill out an occasional missing-persons report. I'll get you some dog tags. We'll get you an ankle bracelet. So I can find you on a GPS if you turn up in some airport." That familiar old word— the one starting with *l* and ending with *ove*, that famous little word so easily turned into a prostitute in popular songs but in fact almost never used by actual poets, unless under suspicion— I'd used it right there in that first sentence. It was printed magnetically in the air like the info on a credit card's brown strip. The word had, of course, never yet come up so far: it was perfect that it should make its debut in a little sour levity. I bounced on the mattress, to roll away and go get the Champagne. Forget about Century 21. There's a wonderful popular expression, *Fuck 'em*. I wasn't going to let my mediocrity as a realtor in a separate life ruin this. I got my bare feet on the floor and started dragging the bedclothes, pulling the thin top blanket off the foot of the bed where it was heaped.

This I was able to wrap myself in, to cross the floor decently—fabric thicker than a bedsheet, stretchy—and I hobbled looking virginal, or like Socrates. Thalia said, "You know, religion is going to be a problem between us, John, because as you know I'm a nonbeliever. Basic differences like that don't make a solid foundation."

I was mincing across the room with my legs bound by the blanket, and strangled, too, with the jubilation that kept climbing up inside, because I couldn't have begun to explain, right at that moment, how pleased I was to hear that there might be "problems" between us!—and that, moreover, "solid foundations" should be built! I'd been delivered up to this strange new platform where even Century 21 didn't matter. I got across the floor in my toga, and there outside the door in the corridor was the wheeled cart with the iced Champagne, which I pulled inside, and I pressed the door closed again.

"Do they still have exorcisms, though?"

I made a show of sagging—my punched-in-the-stomach comedy, to indicate this was a dreary explanation to have to make, pushing my cart back across the floor. "You know, when you're dealing with symbol and myth and liturgy and so on, rational thinking goes right out the window. It's supposed to. It's got to. Different world." Fast as Houdini, I can get out of literal thinking.

She said, "I'd actually feel *better* with a GPS bracelet," in soft astonishment, speaking mostly to herself. As a general idea, it was about as remote and amusing to her as the topic of exorcisms.

"People need their little ceremonies. That's all a minister does." I parked the room service cart by the bed. "An old doctrine is, *everybody* who's baptized is already a 'priest.' Everybody can do the absolve-bless-consecrate thing. Those are the three offices with ordination." I lifted the dewy Champagne bottle out of its ice. I held it up dripping. "It's just, most people do it without a big conscious cosmic, political . . ." I didn't know where that thought was headed. "Which is why I quit the parish." (As I spoke, the old metaphorical picture came back to mind: the word *God* had come to stand as a statue between me and the open sky.) "But in answer to your question, yes, every diocese has an exorcist on call. Archaic thing. Though I couldn't tell you, frankly, if the Northern California diocese exorcist has had a lot of work to do lately. Or ever. In the diocese in L.A. you can go down and take a little short course, to get a certificate. A friend of mine at school did the course, for some reason. So, yes, the archaic stuff is still in there."

"What do *you* like to bless? Most recently, say?"

So now she was taking a warm personal interest in this kooky topic. I sat down on the edge of the bed, in my wrapped-around bedsheet, and I set the Champagne bottle on my thigh to start plucking at the foil on top. The last thing I remembered having fond pastoral feelings about was an old dog. My elderly widowed neighbor across the street has a poodle so old its hair is thinning badly. It's also blind; it sleeps on the woman's hemp doormat all day in faith and in guardianship. The dog was the only thing that came to mind, as an instance of when I'd felt there were forces at work around me bigger than I could comprehend.

"What was the last thing you 'blessed'?"

She was persisting.

"I'll tell you what I'm often *unable* to do, in my frailty," I said. "The *'absolving'* thing is often quite beyond me. Some kid in a BMW cuts me off in traffic. Fuck him. No absolution for him."

"Well, *you* drive a BMW."

"Well, exactly. It's easier to absolve far-away murderers in the news, Hitler and Stalin and Kissinger, the infanticide woman in the tabloids. People in the tabloids generally. I absolve them all. Or what I'm doing technically is *asking* that they *might* be absolved, by higher powers, so I don't have to do it. And I do a lot of 'consecration,' that's pretty constant, that's just knee-jerk. I do it all the time. I do it constantly." I raised up the symbolic Champagne bottle: alcoholism and consecration go nicely together, particularly in that most gluttonous, most bibulous, worldly institution. At a breakfast table alone, or lifting a drippy burger to my mouth at my BMW's steering wheel, a crumpled, elided ceremony of consecration always blows past, as one wishes he were useful to bigger and better forces. The incessant ABC-ing serves to turn *me* off and make me stupid and keep me dully grounded, for example at times like this, tonight, when unbelievable happiness might totally destabilize and derange me, crossing the room wrapped in a bedcover in a Napa resort. On the Champagne cart was a card on heavy paper-stock engraved: WITH OUR COMPLIMENTS. I handed it to her. "This proves they think we're newlyweds," I said. "They don't do complimentary Champagne for sordid booty calls."

It had been a topic of conjecture all afternoon, while we drove from winery to winery: Did the Silverado staff think we were newlyweds. Or just a businessman with his mistress. She took the card and made an affirmative noise, "Mnyp. Wedding bells are engraved on the corners."

The Champagne cork's wire basket could be loosened with a little methodical untwisting. But after I got it off, the stuck, bulging plug, which is quite scary, didn't immediately pop out. The cork fiber itself was rock hard from repressing the explosive wine inside. I'm not very experienced with Champagne.

"And little lovebirds, too," said Thalia. She brought the card close to her eye, because she'd taken out her contacts. "They're carrying lengths of ribbon in their little beaks."

Nest building, of course, would be the symbolism there with those ribbons, a common old motif, though I've never thought of it till now.

I was prying at the cork, wincing, and hiding my face, because there's no guarantee that the projectile will necessarily fire straight out at the ceiling; it might sometimes misfire and shoot diagonally, right at the eye. I was able to work it out by increments with an upward rubbing of both thumbs, and when it did pop and hit the ceiling, my face was turned altogether around in the opposite direction. Anticlimactically, there was no orgasmic gush. It just exhaled its little fume.

Meanwhile Thalia, having contemplated the nest building of the two lovebirds, had started digging through her night bag, and she came up with a light-blue case. It was a case I recognized—made to hold a dental retainer—which I knew because it was precisely the same as mine, both gifts of the orthodontist on the team at the Auctor clinic. My own was at the bottom of my Dopp kit in the bathroom. I hadn't planned on getting it out. I guess I'd thought that, on this one unrealistic magical night we might dispense with the retainers. And pretend they didn't exist.

But Thalia's unconstraint made me feel freer, so I decided, after our little toast, I could get out my own device. We could install our fixtures in our mouths, once we'd had a goodnight kiss, and then roll away—or roll together—most fraternally to sleep for the first time in our lives in a kind of vindication.

THE NEXT DAY began with the sun, like a complimentary bran muffin, already standing free of the Napa Valley hills as it radiated through the still-open French doors leading to the hot tub on the deck; the Champagne bottle in its bucket of water; our clammy bathing suits lying dead on the carpet; and the arrival of yet another room service cart; and under the sheets a certain amount of teenage teasing and nipping and swapping about and lingering, both of us slightly aware that we were acting in imitation of what normal people have always done easily; and then packing our suitcases to check out, to meet up with our seven developmentally disabled adults on Dr. Auctor's property in Sonoma County. Every moment in that room had a distinct feeling of being formally staged for the fulfillment of dreams and for the setting of precedents almost contractually. We are both serious people. A seriousness was something we recognized in each other. That she and I had been transformed into husband and wife, via a single night at a fantasy hotel, would provide useful roles for us during the rest of that day, Sunday, when, together *in loco parentis*, we would face the problem of Francesca's going into labor, right out on the job site, on the hoed dirt beneath Dr. Auctor's tall hedges of English laurel: we discovered her hunkered down on her hands and knees—or rather on her knees and one hand—while her other hand dug at her waistband trying to peel down the red sweatpants she wore, with a cartoon image of handlebar-moustachioed Yosemite Sam emblazoned on the butt, aiming his two huge sixguns out at the world. Thalia and I would be the only mature adults on the scene. The Green Thumbs van that morning, containing its crew, had been driven up from San Rafael, by Sandy (who like a good pal was quietly collaborating in the scheme of getting her girlfriend Thalia laid for once, at last). The general plan for the morning was, Thalia and I were to drive over from Napa and meet the Green Thumbs vehicle at the front gate of Dr. Auctor's country property in Sonoma. Then I was to hand my car over to Sandy, who would drive it back to the San Rafael office. Thalia and I were to spend the afternoon with the Seven Samurai (another of their team names) tending the gardens.

That part of the plan did go smoothly. Sandy stayed in touch with us by cell phone, the whole way up. (On the cell phone connection, George's voice could be heard coming sharply through, from the rear passenger seat where he made regular announcements about Bosco.) Thalia and I hadn't waited at the doctor's front gate for more than five minutes when Sandy showed up to exchange the bus full of clients for my empty German luxury car.

That front gate was going to be the great complicating factor, on this day. It was an impressive barrier, a thick horizontal rod of steel, as fat as a telephone pole. It looked like it weighed many tons. Once Thalia had entered a code into the keypad, in sliding open it made a noise like the scraping blade of a bulldozer. After that success in opening, the gate did allow Sandy to leave, driving away with my car, but thereafter it closed and never opened again, locking us in the estate for the duration of the power failure. These were remote woods in the Sonoma foothills. After leaving the main road we had gone for a mile or two on a gravel drive until it dead-ended at this gate; the geographical layout made me think we must have been traveling on Dr. Auctor's property for most of that distance.

So while the gate was still openable, both the van and my own car came in. We all parked at the gardener's shed, and the clients debouched from the van; Sandy took my car back out the drive, bound for the San Rafael office, with the assurance that the heavy bar would retract automatically as the car approached. The gate did work for Sandy, obviously, because she didn't come back. But it never worked again that day. Thalia and I and the seven clients were stuck inside until electricity was restored during the regional power-grid failure of that October weekend. When Thalia discovered Francesca in obvious labor under the English laurels, crouching forehead-to-ground like a Muslim in prayer, and pushing with a hooked thumb at her elastic waistband—and when Francesca admitted that the pains had been coming with some frequency now—we got everyone in the big van and tried to exit by the gate, but it wouldn't move. We made an attempt at backing up and charging at it again, to trip the sensors, but it stayed still. Thalia got out of the van and ducked under the bar to go out on the road, and she punched the entry code into the key-pad. But still it lay heavily and forbade us to leave. It was the only exit. And both sides of the gate were crowded with impassable trees. And a chain-link fence climbed and descended steep road-side slopes. It wasn't until we called a locksmith, via cell phone, that we learned the power was out all over. We couldn't get a phone connection at several locksmiths' numbers, and then when a locksmith finally did answer, she told us she was no expert on high-security gates; she probably wouldn't come out even if there *were* electrical power. Those gates were for specialized techni-cians. Anyway it sounded to her like such a gate, to be repaired, would need power. Which wasn't to be had, anywhere in North-ern California.

So, back up at the house, we made Francesca comfortable. This was in a den we broke into. And we started trying hospi-tals and police. Hospitals and police were all busy on other more urgent calls, for this was the October day of the Oregon substa-tion failure that knocked out power in a region of three states.

We did continue to have landline phone service at Dr. Auctor's place, but it did us little good; we still couldn't summon any emergency help—a mother's having contractions every few minutes was not so pressing an emergency as some of the other problems that police and rescue services were solving. There is a considerable medical establishment in these rural neighborhoods up in Sonoma County, with plenty of hospitals and clinics, but since they were all operating only partially, on the limited power of their generators, in the triage system our lesser drama was set aside.

The police switchboard, when we called, was glad to hear from us, because their alarm had been satellite-triggered when we jimmied open a window at Dr. Auctor's estate, setting off the automatic security system. (The security system was battery-backed-up.) (Unlike the gate, evidently.) So the police, in this way, had been made aware of a break-in, but their hands were already full with the kinds of calamities that come up in a power outage: traffic lights had stopped functioning and so on; burglar alarms were triggered in malls and homes. They were glad to be informed that we were *not* housebreakers, but our calling did nothing to make them come sooner; it actually moved us down toward the bottom of their priority list. They only told us to keep the patient comfortable. "An hour or two" seemed to be the general estimate for the delay in our rescue, whether by hospital ambulance or police patrol car, and we were told to just hang on. An hour seemed like an endurable time. Francesca meanwhile, where she lay, between contractions looked pretty happy, if sheepishly so. The other clients were all outside together on Dr. Auctor's veranda; sensing the trouble, they grew solemn and tended to bunch nearer each other.

Thalia shut off her cell phone and put it away. I suggested (for this was something we'd joked about earlier) that maybe it was time, now, to go looking in Dr. Auctor's wine cellar. Thalia didn't have a sense of humor at this moment. She only cast her eyes up, and her pretty mouth delved sideways. Being inside Dr. Auctor's home made her uncomfortable. We'd entered through a casement window, and we'd laid Francesca out on a couch in a den that overlooked a long lawn and a flagstone patio. In the presence of Dr. Auctor's personal possessions—books, art objects—a little teasing gag about drinking his wine did feel slightly vandalistic, regrettably.

"There's 9-1-1 for *Napa* County," I said. "Maybe Napa isn't as busy or tied-up as Sonoma. It's farther, but . . ."

Thalia then touched my shoulder and turned away to summon me out into the passageway. To have a private conference.

I followed, loving the marriedness of the moment. The attached room was a kitchen. Or not quite a kitchen but a connecting pantry, whose shelves were filled with books and little sculptures.

When we got out there together, she gave one glance backward toward our Seven, and she said, "Francesca was scheduled for a Caesarean."

She went on looking at me. The meaning of the statement was plain and clear. But its exact consequences, for us and our situation, were slow to take shape in my mind.

"She has an incompetent uterus. That's what it's called medically. And she was"—her hand made a flipping-pages gesture—"scheduled for a Caesarean."

"Has she gone the whole nine months?" The girl hadn't looked extremely pregnant. At least not to my eye.

"Forty weeks is what you want. That's full term. Thirty-eight weeks is what she's done."

"Give or take a couple weeks," I said. Such estimates are usually fuzzy.

"No. Everybody knows the exact date of conception. I do. Because it happened on my watch. The exact date of conception was, ah—you could say—a memorable day for all of us."

"We'll walk!" I said, in happiest seriousness because it dawned as all too plain. "We could walk out. Just go under the gate and go out the road, and hitch a ride. We can get to the highway. She can walk."

Actually Francesca couldn't walk. When I started picturing it, it wasn't going to work. She'd barely hobbled to the house. The distance to the paved road was two miles. Then there would be another two or three miles' hike, to a big-enough road where we might catch a ride. Francesca couldn't do it. She had had a hard time getting up the shallow flagstone stairs and into the house, after I'd crawled through the window and come around to open the patio doors for everybody. I started to imagine myself finding a wheeled conveyance of some kind and carting her up the gravel road. A garden cart or a wheelbarrow might carry the girl: her pretty, blue, serene, Down-syndrome, wide-set eyes could watch the world go by from a wheelbarrow. But I didn't voice that idea aloud, not just yet, and in fact—since it was probably at least an hour's journey, by wheelbarrow, to the highway—I was going to let that whole picture stay unannounced. Here I was, looking into the face of the Thalia I'd first glimpsed six months ago and dismissed as unattainable, but now we could converse like close partners. In her restless gaze, as she worked her imagination, I saw something I took comfort in: a preoccupied briskness; an independence of judgment; which I name "objectivity" and "emotional stability" and "rationality." This was an important thing to consider—her presumptive rationality—because, as I say, I tend to have a weakness for dramatic females, and, moreover, I knew this secret about her now, that she had once had an episode of— as one might think of it—mental illness. She'd once been "not herself," when the rapture of dissociative fugue had overtaken her. You watch the face of a woman you may love as if some revelation might evolve there, lively as a flame on the hearth, but that face—Thalia's is oval, smoothly shaped, framed by the poking brackets of her haircut—a human face is just a social institution we share, a face is a badge, beauty a social device, and monstrous in that way, as is the policeman's brass shield, the priest's pillorying white collar, the leper's smirk, the hag's scowl, all the dramatis personae—and beauty for a woman in society seems a kind of job of work, over the long haul. If you've got it, it will condemn you to certain kinds of undertakings and responsibilities and powers during a lifespan. Thalia had it—she really had the essential thing *before* her lip repair—and she seemed to take naturally to the vocation; beauty suited her like a second skin, which she could ignore, and I felt I could trust her.

I seem so knowledgeable and philosophical, so analytic. I'm such a philosopher, maybe, only because I'm so inexperienced, perpetually analytic of woman, because woman was always unattainable. My intimacies, as I've said, transpired mostly while I wore the costume of cleric. So I will have been "catnip to" only a certain sort of female parishioner, who, given the whole setup—the harelip and the white collar—might have been a maladjusted female parishioner indeed. I can think of one particular parishioner who, in the rectory office, crossed the room and knelt down on the floor before my chair and grasped my thighs to tell me about her compulsions to sin. My expression of prim horror kept my chin above those rising waters. An extremely common maneuver of women—that is, those who stay across the room in the opposite chair—is to confide with casual nonchalance the most sexually explicit situations they've experienced. Or imagined. They go on and on. A number of women do this. I hear this from other men, too; it's an apparently universal tactic of flirtation. Perhaps two or three times a year, I would have to hear accounts of women's anatomical preferences, or little homoerotic skirmishes, atrocious delights, confessions of their pining to try something they'd learned of by watching *precisely* the sorts of Internet video clips I myself had secret knowledge of. In these interviews, the level of specificity, the ongoing narrative coherence, was always such that, clearly, half the motive was to cause the hard pain in me. Yet I was never in danger of crossing the office floor myself—I always stayed in my own chair, the tilt-back leather desk chair I still own—finishing the conversation always with a double-handed handshake, or a chaste hug, *after* the office door had been reopened and the church secretary was out there, her back turned, working at her dusty outdated computer while her radio played soft rock—I was protected from temptation by the lip. In temptation, I would always have to imagine a kiss—imagine *myself* kissing—and that barrier stopped me. In the centuries before the Reformation, the Catholic institution was constantly in trouble on account of priestly philandering, and I personally know the particular reason. The reason is that the sacrament of confession used to take place without a screen between sinner and confessor. This was during the whole first thousand years of the institution. So a village priest, in the old days, had to sit face-to-face in privacy with a parishioner describing impure thoughts or deeds. And surely they weren't all envy or sloth or gluttony. The consequences were inevitable. After the church introduced the lattice to stand between them, the problem abated. The modern Protestant minister, in his office with the door closed against his secretary, is in the same predicament as the ancient Catholic. To sit knee-to-knee with a woman who is confiding her worries, and her adventures, creates an emotional bond. In other words, people come to truly respect each other, and understand each other, and think of each other fondly. As it matures, it is a bond that chaste abstinence strangles to dangerous euphoria. Those days were blissful. Some of those women adored me more than their husbands, their problematic husbands. (Husbands, poor husbands, by nature problematic.) There were days I was walking on air.

So my few strictly romantic entanglements, as edited by my priestliness, may have involved only a certain kind of woman, a woman particularly interested in inciting desire in a cleric. A dog-lipped cleric, yet! (to add to the image of the white neckmanacle implying God's Great Leash). Maybe it was a Beauty-and-the-Beast psychology. Or maybe I appealed to women of a nurse's constitution. In my disguise of black cloth, they saw me as lonely and, of course, profound.

Therefore, here was the essential terror of the gaze I was sharing with Thalia. It was only my own new-sculpted mask that had equipped me for love's consummation, love's confession. As I looked at the face of the woman I was saying I loved, I was a stranger to myself. Which I'd really always been.

For I have a kind of parallel affliction to Thalia's episode of dissociative fugue: it's that I have never had a "gift," or a reason for living. I'm like an anonymous supernumerary in the world. I'm still waiting; that is, waiting for a reason. Plenty of people have this—this is no great "existential angst" of any kind—and compared to Thalia's onetime debilitating mental dysfunction, I know my problems aren't dramatic; I thrive always in the assurance that my existence does have the high purpose all of us have, of mysteriously fulfilling God's love. That's indeed a truism; it risks being platitudinous and unhelpful, and I've seen "God's love" be *cruelly* platitudinous and unhelpful in cases much worse than mine. Rather, I suffer from a lack of a personal, particular fate. Most commonly, one takes up the priesthood not because one has been "called" in some dramatic numinous way but, more often than not, as a way of *asking* to be called and *wishing* one had been called, hoping for it, for a genuine vocation. You pretend, but you're pretending in order to, maybe, make the real thing come along eventually. The psychology of a fifteen-year old boy is, no doubt, complicated and unmappable—a boy intelligent but lonely, still lacking in all the habitual emotional glues and stickinesses that sustain decision making in more mature people. In high school, the only kind of glue I remember having, to hold me together, was competitive swimming, the fifteen-hundred-meter freestyle, the long hours in those cruel echoes and chlorine and buoyant self-sufficiency. I'm pretty sure I wanted to put on the robes of a vocation at that age because, inwardly, I had always felt myself to be like a kind of unnumbered coin, a coin without any imprint or denomination, issued perhaps mistakenly, or just fallen from the tables of enumeration, a blank disk or chip or marker. I lacked a personality. This all may have had to do with my badly minted face. I had no gift. Mahalia Jackson's gift is to sing. A policeman's gift is to keep order. Winston Churchill's is to lead. Charlie Chaplin's is to make people laugh. The New Testament offers a little catalogue of gifts to be put to work in the world: teaching, healing, interpretation of tongues, learning, et cetera. It trivializes my shortcoming to say, for example, that I can't sing or play an instrument or dance, or that when I try my hand at art, all my drawings and sketches turn out looking like the same moronic treasure map, or that, in the great art galleries and museums of the world, my eye is bored and parched, or that, as a writer, even my sermons were sometimes (especially toward the end) written with the help of the patented CD-ROM "Text and Tradition," or even Wesley's Standard Sermons. Or even downloaded from PreachIt.org, which has a vast selection of free downloadable homilies on thousands of texts and topics— not in order to plagiarize them wholesale (I exonerate myself to that degree), but to go fishing for an idea, a theme, an inspiration, and maybe outright steal a little of the language, if it's any good.

Since the surgery, I no longer have the excuse of deformity—or "gift" of deformity, because that's what it was. I'm pretending now more than ever—pretending, that is, to know why I'm alive. And the pretense is the more obvious to me, and the more obvious to the world. I'm forty-nine now. As I looked into her eyes, in Dr. Auctor's kitchen, I was only a stand-in for a man eligible for love. Because a man has to bring something. I wasn't bringing anything. She didn't know that about me, yet. The sum of what I have is a portfolio of little investments and a paid-off house in a nice San Rafael neighborhood. And a car and a closetful of clothes.

It was the most ill-chosen moment, but I wanted to say something right then, in my weakness, to confess that I needed or wanted her. I began, "Thalia, we really haven't known each other long."

That, I realized, sounded like a preamble to a marriage proposal.

And sometimes things might be, exactly in the end, what they seem like.

Then she inadvertently rescued me, by reaching across, patting my forearms (they were folded hard upon my chest), and crying, "John! Yes! We'll call a cab! Why didn't we think of that? We can call a cab."

ALL MY TORMENTS of self-doubt were, in Thalia's universe, *totally invisible*. Thalia's eyes—brown, with flaws of amber—were laid open to mine, and mine open to hers, yet she didn't see the Kingdom of Doubt inside me, its towers and walls and palaces and pagodas, its highly developed system of growth and colonization, infrastructure, foreign policy, information ministry, foreign-aid programs, et cetera, et cetera. This abstraction "Satan" has a wonderful pertinence; I've come to have a respect for the old cartoon, cloven-hoofed and infinitely resourceful, because, for instance, right at that moment, my loyalty to the Kingdom of Doubt proved stronger than love. I wanted her to see my self-doubt and mistrust me as a matter of practical precaution, because standing before her, my new disguise has an unintended effect of *transparency*. The risk of actually being loved was too great.

However, the idea of calling a cab was immediately postponed because there was a noise, and when we looked back at the den, where Francesca lay on her couch, her water had broken. I knew right away. It was obvious. A fresh dithering alarm broke out among her bedside friends. Most of them, now, had ventured into the sacred and terrible vicinity of her. But suddenly they backed away from her, with the exception of Tony—he was the discoverer and announcer of this new development, and he couldn't contain his uproarious hilarity.

So calling a cab seemed less feasible. At the point when the water is broken, doesn't the mother begin to consider herself down for the count? Also, her clothes were wet now, yes, and this new trouble—all its practical considerations, like the pants' removal and then the need to find a blanket or sheet to keep her decent—was going to stick Francesca down in place here now. This was, increasingly, going to be the place where she lay down.

Nevertheless, I did start trying, calling around for cabs. I left the room to make the calls, carrying Dr. Auctor's cordless phone—it had a dial tone despite the power outage. I looked at it; the manufacturer was VTech, and it must have had an auxiliary battery.

So I told the four males, "Come on, all you men, we're going to make a phone call," and I herded them out. This way, Francesca could be freed from her Yosemite Sam sweatpants. I ended up contacting every cab and limo in the area directory, while we men all stood in a group in the kitchen. There were three cab companies. One of them had the promising name of North Bay Transport and Wheelchair, but that one turned out to be closed on Sundays. There were also two "chartered tour" services in Sonoma. Everybody I reached was too busy and told me it might be an hour before they could send a car at all. Auctor's house was far from town; the round trip itself would require an hour. Our problem was, we would probably need someone sooner than an hour. That was becoming unmistakable. My conversations with dispatchers became more choppy and distracted because I could hear Francesca's cries of pain. We all could. The perpetrator, Tony, just kept grinning with brilliant shame during each cry. George's way of registering discomfort was a lot like his friend Veevee's: the pulse point of his wrist would press against his neck, or ear, and soon his whole forearm would be sawing against his ear. The word *incompetent*, when applied to a uterus, seems to imply the opening is closed, or at least straitened, and it was dawning on me that we could be facing a death here, on a sunny afternoon, birdsong in the trees, butterflies in the peonies. My imagination had not yet gone to the extreme point of picturing a rude abdominal incision, to rescue a live baby from a dead mother. I'm not a ready man, in an emergency. In an emergency I tend to stay out of the way to make it easy for other (brave or knowledgeable) people, to do what needs to be done, for I'm aware that the absolve-bless-consecrate business, which used to be my specialty, is to many people relevant and consequential but often doesn't seem that way.

I stayed in the kitchen waiting for a quiet lull between contractions. Then when, having failed to get a cab, I brought my four orange-vested men back into the room, the patient was decently covered up, her knees under the tent of a knitted afghan shawl, actually smiling, in her mild way, at her friends. Thalia had left the bedside—the couchside—to go across to the wall of the den and pick through Dr. Auctor's liquor cabinet, returning with a bottle of vodka, to administer a dose to Francesca. Oscar, as soon as he saw the vodka, complained, "I get some. What is it?" I was starting to love Oscar, in his predictability.

Thalia said, "You wouldn't like it. It's vodka. Haven't you tasted booze before? You really wouldn't like it. It's booze."

George, too, was as jealous as Oscar. "I love booze."

"You do not, George. Now, Francesca, sit up a little bit. This stuff doesn't taste great, but it will make you feel relaxed." While she tipped a little vodka into a glass, she asked me, "Do you think I'm doing the right thing here?"

I didn't really have an opinion. It seemed like an all right idea to me. All I said was, "Maybe I'll wander around a little. See if there's anything."

Nothing particular was in my mind. Just some resource, some tool, some communication device, anything we could use. Or maybe something to stimulate an idea. Or an emergency key for the outer gate. Maybe the outer gate did have a back-up battery. "The one dispatcher said they could have a cab free in sixty minutes. He was the only one who would promise. So I told them okay. I said we'd meet him at the gate. Sixty minutes plus a little: maybe you can get her to hold out for sixty minutes, and maybe the cops will be here then."

Throughout all this, the clients were behaving with restraint. Tony was the only one who might have had a tendency to be obstreperous, but Tim had censured him, telling him not to be a tard. There was George's and Oscar's jealousy of the vodka. And there was Veevee's angry lament that they'd ever left the Green Thumb offices this morning: she'd spoken the same way yesterday; apparently she made the same complaint every day. But mostly, in this emergency, the clients sensed that this was serious and they stayed together in a close group, standing up, not sitting down on the doctor's furniture, not touching anything at all, keeping their hands to themselves. They were frightened as well as awed by what had come to pass because of Tony's and Francesca's famous fooling around.

I was in the kitchen, looking around vaguely for an inspiration. Dr. Auctor was a bachelor and his home was a low fortress of glass and stacked flagstones, with furniture and counters and built-in shelves, all shrunken to make a tiny man comfortable. I hadn't noticed it till now. I hadn't focused on why I'd felt like an intruding bear. The kitchen counters were more like table height. The cupboards had a dollhouse feeling. The whole place was specially designed for a four-foot man.

One idea then crossed my mind. I called into the den, "I could phone a tractor, Thalia. Like a bulldozer or a heavy-equipment operator. Somebody could *smash* through the gate, maybe."

Actually, it didn't seem likely. The heavy log of steel stretching across the driveway, anchored on either side by cast-cement blocks, looked like something that could withstand a bulldozer. The shiny great cylinder was jacketed in a patina of delicate rust that, somehow chemically, implied tonnage. And when we'd been out trying to open it, I'd touched it and felt how deeply cold it was, with the chill of the immovable.

I carried on, though, "Maybe a building contractor or a heavy-equipment operator would be in the Yellow Pages. They could send out a tractor. If their office is open on Sunday."

Thalia didn't answer, then she said, absently, "Mm, good idea."

My next idea was that the gate could be exploded. With dynamite or something. Some kind of pyrotechnician could be found in the phone book.

This idea, though, I didn't mention at all.

There was a certain door beside the refrigerator in the kitchen, which seemed interesting because it would be an odd place to attach a room. It was too heavy a door to be a closet. When I opened it, it led to a dark windowless space, annexed to the kitchen by another short passageway. I flipped the light switch on the wall and I got no light, forgetting there was a power failure. But the room seemed worth investigating: judging by the acoustics that came to my ear, and the air mass that rose against my face, I could tell it was a big place with carpet and furniture, but it was windowless.

A flashlight was what I needed, and I went back and looked in the kitchen cupboards. The same template exists in all our middle-class minds for the practical furnishing of a home, and on my first try, the drawer beside a broom closet exposed a red plastic flashlight. A flashlight would be useful in general, if we were to be stranded in a power outage.

Still not knowing what I was seeking—maybe the secrets of the front security gate's emergency override, or something like an instruction manual, or any useful resources, a bottle of sedatives for the patient, or possibly some kind of tool or method of exit I could never have thought of—I went back to the passageway. It led to a low-ceilinged carpeted room, without windows. My flashlight beam flipped around the walls. But I shouldn't have been looking. Forbiddenness was here. There were taxidermy-stuffed pets on shelves, and large jars of floating pickled animals. I wished I hadn't opened that door. Before my eye had alighted,

I had gone instinctually blind with the swarming tingle of tres-
pass and dread, yet I had to go on looking rather than turn away.
Because there I was. One large thing, standing on a shelf, was
the stuffed body of a dog, but the dog looked to be partly fowl.
I tried to figure it out from where I stood in the doorway, not
wanting to get closer to anything. The animal had been shaved
all over, so a pallid goose-pimpled skin formed its surface. The
strange thing was, its rear legs were like barnyard fowl's legs, like
the wrinkly legs of a roast turkey before it goes in the oven. This
was the outcome of plastic surgery. They were dog's legs but rede-
signed and hairless. Its thigh bones had somehow been elided, or
they'd been detached from the hip sockets and reattached at new
places closer to the shoulders of the animal, so the thighs looked
bunched. That was what gave it the fowl-like look. Whatever had
been done to it, the animal had evidently survived the operation,
and even possibly used the reattached legs to move and walk,
because it was clear that the whole transplant and its incisions
had healed over.

The moving flashlight kept me standing there. On the shelf
beside the stuffed dog was a cat, mounted on a board, oddly tall.
Its front legs had some kind of extensions, which I did not want
to linger on, but my flashlight kept reverting to it. It was as if
stilted. It resembled a statue of an Egyptian cat-goddess. In its
immortality, this creature's eyes were closed, unlike the dog's.
Further along the shelf there were immense jars of clear fluid
where amphibious-looking things ballooned; one thing as big
as a football seemed as if it might be a frog. In another jar was
a kind of hairless fetal scrawny thing, tumbling and spiraling
slow as a galaxy in its little sealed-off eternity. At that point,
something childish in me was scared of being in the room and
I did go back out. And closed the door, and in my superstitious
shiver I got as far as halfway across the kitchen, then I more
maturely slowed down. Dr. Auctor was simply an experimenter
of some kind. This wasn't the moment to mention my discovery
to Thalia. The patient was lying on the couch making whim-

pers in gasps, eyes stitched shut, her complexion worrisome now. The four orange-vested men had been sent outside. On the patio they were gathered together looking out over the estate grounds, standing in a row in their waiting-for-a-bus attitudes. Thalia was on her cell phone.

"Who are you calling?"

"Just a minute." She removed the phone from her ear and punched a numeral. Then she went back to listening.

I said, "Don't use up your cell phone. Use the regular phone. It's probably got better batteries."

She said, "Yes, hi, we're patients of Dr. Auctor's, and I know he's in Switzerland right now, but it's very important that we reach him. I know. Yes. Or someone who would know how to reach him there."

"Oh," I told Thalia. "Good idea."

I wasn't mentioning the news that Dr. Auctor had seemed to make a hobby of experimental surgery on pets. And I supposed I would go on not mentioning it. There might be nothing sinister about it. Those could be legitimate specimens from legitimate studies of some kind. There might be good reasons, or therapeutic reasons, for moving a dog's legs forward. Though probably not for adding an extra joint extension to a cat's front legs.

Thalia held the phone away from her ear—she seemed to have been put on hold—and she asked me, "I'm doing this, so would you get the lunches? From the van? And take Veevee and Susan out to help? And go ahead and distribute them around, because they'll all be hungry. The lunches are in the cardboard box in back." Even while she spoke, I was headed for the door, grateful to be getting away from the bedside of pain. Susan and Veevee were following. Thalia added, "The lunch bags have everybody's name on them, but they're all the same. Except for Tim's. All Tim's food is in plastic lidded things. Make sure Tim gets his."

It was good to get outside in the air and away from Francesca's misery. As we left she was going into another contraction, and her eyes had a way of whiting up during each contraction.

There wasn't much vocal complaint from her at this point, only gasps of breath. And then, at each recovery, she smiled. The four men outside on the patio looked, each, personally guilty of all this misery, except for Tony, who looked proud, if a bit edgily.

I said, "It's time to get into our lunch bags, folks," heading for the van.

None of the men responded. But Veevee and Susan went with me to open the rear door.

Veevee said, tattling, "George already ate his whole lunch."

Developmentally disabled adults, after the novelty wears off, can sometimes be a depressing—or just tiring—group to spend time with, partly because (I decided this as I carried the box of lunch bags, remembering the feeling I used to get during the Special Olympics volunteering I used to do in Los Angeles) there's an unashamed selfishness on display often, among retarded adults, which one never sees in grown-ups, or at least not so openly undisguised. With certain exceptions. Francesca for example. Poor Francesca was a generous, unselfish soul; it shone forth in the way she smiled in relief between contractions. Every other client seemed mostly always to wait, glumly or opportunistically, for the next development that would directly concern himself.

"Want to do it to a tard?" Tim asked me in a grim murmur as I came back with the box of lunch bags to the standing row of men on the patio. The wisecrack made Tony laugh in shame, and blush. The other two men looked only worried by such vulgarity. Especially Oscar. Oscar couldn't believe such things were sayable: he looked privately horrified, and his cheek blotches came out. Tim explained, "Tony'll do it," with disgust.

George realized that the lunches were here, and he demanded, "Is there Bosco?"

"George, is it true that you've eaten your lunch?" I said. I could see there were only six paper bags in the box. Yesterday, the lunches had been entrusted individually to the clients. Today they'd been stored together in a box to prevent Susan from setting up her granola-bar brokerage again. I supposed if George were hungry, we would have to look into Dr. Auctor's cupboards to feed him. Getting into Dr. Auctor's cupboards was perhaps inevitable, if we were to be stranded for some while. Or getting into the freezer, where presumably things were now thawing.

Tony was displeased with the withdrawal of attention from himself, and with a grin he told everybody, "I do it."

"George gets an extra lunch!" Oscar complained, his fingertips nipping at each other beneath his chin in his envy.

The first real cry of pain came through the plate glass of the den. A cry of a whole different order, it was almost a surprised or delighted sound, oddly, like laughter.

Then Thalia appeared in the doorway, folding her cell phone. "I called Sandy. She's perfect. 'Cause she knows how to get here. She knows the way."

"Oh," I said. "Good idea. Of course."

"She'll come up, but it will take *her* a long time, too, of course. She doesn't know anybody in Sonoma County either. So we'll see. Either the cab will get here first or Sandy will."

"Good idea," I repeated, in a sort of bewilderment, because why hadn't I thought of calling any number of people back in Marin? Or whether I might happen to know anybody up here?

Which I didn't anyway, however. Nobody came to mind in Sonoma County.

"Also I reached Bim. He's going to phone back—he's in Zurich—but the first thing he said was, the vodka was sort of a mistake, but it'll be okay. And he said Francesca might not *have* an hour. Like really. He's got better drugs for her, here in the house. But he's going to make a list of everything we'll need and he's going to call back."

I knew of course what she meant. We were going to deliver a baby, an operation in which, with my ABC skills, I would look pretty useless, unless something went wrong, and even then useless.

SO RIGHT AWAY I shrank to an unreasonable child, because I didn't care if she thought I was a coward; I just wasn't the brave type, not in medical situations. She would have to forgive me. A woman in travail is a holy beast that a man keeps his distance from unless he is a qualified, gowned surgeon—who oddly is a kind of nongendered, neutered being, and a bit like a priest, in that way, or an exorcist, and he enters chiming with the sanctity of *his* own specialization and education. Not my specialization. Not my department.

However, standing there with the wish to be irresponsible, I faced a further inevitability. I would have no choice. I might not be able to overcome my fear but yet would get through this day somehow anyway.

Delivering a baby presumably takes strength, that is, hand strength and arm strength if things are going poorly, strength that a male possesses—though there are female obstetricians, and I did have an impression that there are tools, things like tongs, to get a grip on a baby's head and get some leverage. The alternative might be a death here if I didn't help. Or two deaths, the mother's and the infant's. The expression "incompetent" probably did mean the uterus was impassable, not just narrow or funny shaped. So there would be cutting on Francesca's belly skin, and at that point I went blandly schizoid: I surrendered to the general feeling that I would put effort into whatever activities were required, as if this were a game without real consequences. Maybe it was like seeing the world through the same weird goggles as those maniacs who spray machine gun bullets over schoolyard crowds with steadfast workmanlike calm in their infrared detachment from reality: such was the frame of mind in which I could watch my own hand incising Francesca's cute belly skin. Thalia had vanished from the doorway with the little grumble, "Do I call him Bim? Or Hieronymus?"

"Bosco," George murmured with a languid relish, and I turned to see—something that hadn't been visible to Thalia— that everyone in the circle was admiring Tony's erection, which he had released from his jeans, an ivory boomerang, forced by its inward pressure into a wrongward bend. He held it up handsfree, so it tapped the Day-Glo orange panels of his plastic safety vest as it floated, his palms uplifted, in the sacramental gesture of beholding the host in amazement. I supposed it was my responsibility, *in loco magistri*, to get him to stuff it away again. I lacked the bravery even for that. I would have preferred to just pretend I hadn't seen; and in a useless irrelevance, I reflected—or at least one may hope—that poor dull low-IQ Francesca had had, maybe, one single minute of bliss/surprise/delight in the Civic Center bushes, when she incurred this terrible mortal trouble. But then, picturing that scene, I could guess that everything for that gentle girl Francesca is a matter of surprise and delight, nothing too exceptional about the surprise of a strange little orgasm. From inside the den—it was time again—a smothered cry went out over Dr. Auctor's gardens.

"Tony, put that away," I said. Neither he nor anybody responded; they were all under the influence of his floating wand. While George actually seemed curious, as if he were warring with an inner impulse to reach out and pet it, Veevee by contrast looked so angry at the thing she seemed ready to spit at it. Her lips were working in that way. Tim turned and confided to me, in a voice meant to be heard by all, "Just tell him you'll tell his mother and Adult Protective Services."

I didn't have to say it. At those words, Tony looked annoyed and betrayed and started cramming it all back in his pants with a lot of torso contortions to make it all fit.

"Would you help with something, John?" said Thalia. She had come back, standing in the doorway embracing two clear plastic flat water bags, the kind that are used in intravenous drips. She'd found them somewhere in Dr. Auctor's house. Apparently, we were going to do this job right. "I need you to move a piece of furniture."

She had completely missed the indecent exposure. But of course such mischief was old hat to her, in this job. So I wouldn't bother mentioning it until later. I came inside. She was saying, "Maybe there's even a coat rack. That would be perfect. I have to put these bags up high. Like hang 'em up. To get gravity. It seems like there's a valve," she'd begun talking mostly to herself now as she moved on. I went to the kitchen and got the flashlight, on the counter where I'd left it. So I could go looking. No coat rack in sight, but there was a closet with wire hangers—and one of those hangers, or several hangers in a chain, could be bent into an apparatus for suspending an IV bag. From a curtain rod.

But I looked out in the den, and on the big windows there was no curtain rod.

Without much thinking, I had my plan. I found a paring knife in a drawer, small and sharp, and I found something heavy to pound it in with: a little stone sculpture from the passageway shelves.

Back in the den, I took up a stance behind Francesca's couch, and as hard as I could, I stabbed the little knife into the wood of the window frame. Then with the stone sculpture (it looked like something Native American, like something from Alaska), I hammered the knife deeper into the wood.

It worked fine. From this, I hung the coat hanger. The IV bag had an obvious hole at the top for hanging it. Thalia was carrying both bags around with her, off to other rooms, where she must have been looking for more medical tools. So I supposed I should just wait beside the patient. *With* the patient.

Then the patient did a sweet thing. She had come up for a moment of better alertness because she was about to plunge into another contraction, and seeing me standing beside her, she smiled and took my hand before closing her eyes and bracing herself. I looked out on the patio deck, holding her hand. No one was there. All the clients had vanished together in a group, but the six lunch bags were there on the bench, unopened. So the clients were somewhere. Probably all together. They could be up to anything, but I didn't want to leave Francesca now.

THALIA ANSWERED ON the first ring when Dr. Auctor called back. It was his own house phone, and she used the cordless from the kitchen, with pen and paper prepared to take notes. She developed a long list. A great collection of tools and accessories would have to be assembled, all to be found here in the house. She seemed to take forever, listening, affirming, soaking up descriptions of scissor blades, drug labels, "hemostatic" clamps (which I knew enough Greek to decipher as blood-stopping clamps), sponges. Meanwhile I drifted back and forth between the kitchen and the den, where the patient needed someone around during her conscious moments between crises.

As well as during the crises. But then, whenever the voltage passed through her, all I could do was stand clear. She'd stopped trying to hold my hand, or wanting to. In her unconscious periods when she almost seemed to go to sleep during lulls, she wasn't relaxed but stiff and tense, her eyes always shut now. She was a very good girl, in her own mind; she'd never done anything to ask for this, and that blamelessness of her own freed her from anguish. When she had had moments of lucidity, she smiled up at me as if to offer *me* comfort and reassurance.

Thalia, her list aflutter, came out of the kitchen and asked, "Where's your flashlight? We have to go fast."

She still didn't know about the botched-looking animals on pedestals and in jars, and as she led me through that dark flashlight-lit room to a further door—a door where Dr. Auctor had directed her—she was too distracted to notice anything. That dog created the medieval figure of a gargoyle looming palely outside the flashlight beam.

The far door of that room led to a further open chamber, windowless as if it were a basement, floored in linoleum with a drain in the center, beige metal shelves and plastic drawers along the walls. This was all the medical equipment we would need. It was all in these cupboards. Thalia, with the flashlight, had gone straight for the refrigerator, to kneel and look inside, poking and sorting.

"He said the expiration date might be past, but he said use it anyway, it's fine." She picked out a couple of little things.

Lacking a flashlight, I was useless in this dark room, so I went back out. "I'm getting a light for myself."

Running the gauntlet past the preserved monsters, I decided instead I ought to go outside and search for the six developmentally disabled adults. At last sighting, they'd all stood hypnotized by Tony's stupid penis. So in a way, I dreaded finding them.

My peculiar deference. It can sometimes look a lot like timidity. If carried far enough, one defers to all human beings' basic intimidating dignity. Even to developmentally disabled adults' basic intimidating dignity. Will Thalia forgive it, or even admire it? Humility—this being enthralled by others' charisma—was surely one of the reasons I left the parish: I'd begun to lose all authority, socially. Authority was replaced by a kind of stupefaction, in the company of other people, a dumbfoundedness before the basic numinosity in physical persons, and a desire only to escape them. Increasingly during my years as a public performer of sacraments, an actual, repellent halo around people was becoming perceptible, the glamour of flesh, the poached-egg smell, the stuff itself. It was of course only a kind of abstract *idea* of a halo, and it was discernible only in the absent—the recollected—men or women, for example only when I contemplated them in the solitude of my rectory. Not when I ran into the actual, appalling *person,* in the supermarket, say, or on a sidewalk, or during the Sunday narthex ordeal. One can love humanity when they're remote. But confronted with an actual standing corpus, this is not just an annoyance with my fellow man's halitosis or tiresome opinions; it's an amazement in standing before a creature. I'm amazed at men's indifference, how they can treat each other like neighboring sacks of potatoes on life's conveyor belt, or like cars side by side at a stoplight, rather than as seraphic beings, mystical beings weaving all time together, within the knot "immediacy." Our indifference to each other seems an incipient *criminal* mentality, a brutal retardedness, near that willingness to spray machine gun fire. In my costume-disguise as a realtor, every workday, I spray that machine gun fire dispassionately, don't I? For a costume is not so much a way of becoming dangerously invisible to the rest of the world; it's most importantly a way of becoming dangerously invisible to *oneself.* As every boy knows, a costume confers impunity and specially licenses wickedness, and so it is with my REALTOR® disguise, just as with the clerical collar I once hid behind. Sunday mornings, of course, used to be an ordeal: three services in a single day—a short eight-o'clock service without even an organist, floorboard creaks as the sole accompaniment, when the furnace hasn't yet quite got the sanctuary warm, preaching to a small handful of the cranky, the ardent, the persnickety, the closely listening, those early birds who will get their worm even on a Sunday; then a nine-o'clock, *with* the addition of organist; then, at ten thirty, the big ninety-minute pageant for late-sleepers, including four hymns and the full choir loft and all the High Church bells-and-smells. During each of these services there came the embarrassing moment called Passing the Peace, a rather recent innovation in the liturgy, when everybody has to turn and shake his neighbors' soft hands, and meet each other's eyes, violating the decent personal privacy that once sealed communicants from each other. Passing the Peace,

during my ministerial days, used to require a lot of glad-handing
from me, stepping off the chancel in my vestments, swimming
out on the floor among the pews with hand outstretched—and
then after each service, there was the crowding toward the door,
and the individualized personal handclasps outside in the sun
as all the parishioners were graduated, one by one, back into
their lives. There, the actual effigy of a fellow mortal—clothed
in flesh, and standing across from me under the glaring light of
our universe's nearest star—grew increasingly into a showdown
I cowered before, this despite all my jaunty self-confidence and
all my unctuous social skills, and despite the shield of harelip.
The divorcée Bette Crayne from the rear pew! Her plucked eye-
brows! Her ten years' attendance! Her ongoing unmarriedness!
And the Mastersons, the sleek childless couple from third pew
right! A middle-aged couple's perfectly blow-dried unisex hair-
styles! Yellow patent leather belt! Suntan! There was old worried
Helen Pinkit from second pew left, who we hoped would leave
her fortune to the church. Her saliva-deprived lips. Her turquoise
jewelry. I was actually tired of these people, so I told myself. The
truth is I feared encountering them. A petty misanthropy was
caused by no defect in them; it was my own defect, my selfish
torpor, my superiority, my reclusiveness, but it was, above all, my
incomprehension. It was only when I considered them *in their
absence* that I saw them in their true form: as emanations of light,
consubstantial with myself, congelation of love, ectoplasm, like
me propped up above the soil and gesturing. Face-to-face, our
flusteredness returns, and all the panoply of self-defense rears up;
if we confront each other accidentally in the frozen-foods section, or on the church steps on Sunday when we say our weekly
good-bye—*good-bye indeed!*—we're all so charismatic, even the
most scorned of us, so that even Tony, with what I've called his
stupid floating penis, rules over a small but logical universe of his
own in which we wiser ones appear in cameo parts as bit players.
Humility, the universal balm, is the one medicine most subversive to apply, as it's a universal solvent, too. The year I became

a real estate agent, my shyness abated. I had something like a vocation. Much better, as a shepherd of souls, to be installing Shawn and Cheese in their 3br/1ba starter, or helping the beautiful talented "Rick Shantih" put his wife, accursed of God, away in jail, or hustling Edna Goodkind off to her little waiting room, 620 sq. ft. with balconette.

SO HAVING RECOGNIZED that I ought to go out in the woods and find Tony and everyone, with instant laxity I decided not to. Whatever was happening out there, I didn't want to know. Anyway the more urgent consideration was Francesca; she would need the full attention of two adults. And honestly it wasn't a matter of my own laxity at all. Between contractions, the canceled expression in her eyes, when they ceased to flutter and came half-open, was looking like death.

"Here, put this on her," said Thalia, returning with her forearms draped in tubes, spilling with gadgets. What she separated out for me was a blood pressure cuff—its rubber stems, its ocean-kelp bulb, its band of black Velcro. "And when you're done, don't take it off. We're just going to keep it on her the whole time and check it sometimes. Do you know how to do blood pressure?" She approached the couch carrying two little white pills in a pinch and knelt to poke them into the unconscious patient. "She gets these."

"What are those?"

"I don't know, I forget."

Francesca let herself be wakened long enough to accept the two pills and a swallow of water.

"So Bim says vodka was the wrong thing."

"Hm," I said. "'Bim.'"

"Dr. Auctor," she said. "He answers his phone and he says 'Bim.' Can you hang up the IV bag? I'm going to try to put this together. It's the thing that pumps anesthetic in." It was a white device with buttons.

The IV bag was heavy. But my paring knife was stuck securely deep in the soft wood of the window frame, and the wire hanger was well suspended there. I hung the bag up by the reinforced hole in the top end—it would be fine, it wasn't that heavy, it said 1000 ML—meanwhile Thalia had been connecting tubes with a Y-splitter. It was fitting that she should be the expert. Being a special-ed teacher is next to being a nurse. Also, her taking all the initiative meant, perhaps, she might be the one lifting a scalpel and making the cuts.

She seemed to read my mind because she said, "You're doing the actual operation, John. Not me. I can't do it. You have to do it."

There was hopeless certainty in her voice. It was definite; she was laying down the law, but things were happening so fast here, I was unable to evaluate whether I had any objection to this course, or would have preferred things otherwise: we were all gushing together over this precipice. I had just finished attaching the blood-pressure cuff when Francesca convulsed with pain and slid down along the couch. The way she arched her back, it made her slide off altogether onto the floor.

"Fine. Leave her on the floor. Better on the floor." Thalia knelt crawling.

I pulled the afghan down from the couch, because the patient was naked from the waist down, while still sporting the orange plastic safety vest.

"Bim said spread newsprint, but . . ."

We wouldn't bother with newsprint. The floor in this den was glossy hardwood.

She was screwing a tube into the side of the little device.

Blood was on the couch where Francesca had lain. I wasn't sure if that was a bad sign or just a normal part of labor and deliv-

ery. But the sight reprinted a conviction in my mind, like a sort
of Rorschach blot that had already existed in my soul: I would
not do any cutting. I did not want to be touching blood or inward
parts. In that case, I would be sitting off to one side in total cra-
ven, stubborn contradiction of Thalia's bidding.

Though it wouldn't provide a permanent evasion, I did plan
to go outside at some point to look for the rest of the clients, out
there somewhere in a circle in the deep woods. I pictured a few
safety vests shed and abandoned along a woodland path. In fact
retarded adults, mostly, seem to have all the usual moral apparatus, of guilt and shame and scruple. But those very same ones,
oddly, can slip into an innocence, where the rules don't apply.
They just forget. Like Jehovah I would have to surprise them and
herd them out of paradise.

Meanwhile I did happen to know how to take blood pressure,
and I had pumped up the bulb and watched the needle descend
through its little inch-long journey of pulses.

"Her blood-pressure seems high, to me," I said. "This is
showing one-ninety over ninety. Do you think that's bad?"

Thalia went on plugging together rubber tubes and didn't
answer. She would have no special knowledge about blood pressure. She could ask the doctor on the next call.

I said, "What is the story with Tim?"

"Tim?" she said.

Knowing exactly the kind of thing I was getting at, she said,
"His IQ is seventy-five. But he's got emotional disorders and
autism. He can be a mean guy." The lengths of IV tubing were
packaged in sterile plastic bags, and she tore open another one.

"I probably ought to go find them, you know," I said. "They've
gone somewhere."

"Tim's an instigator. Wherever they are now, he's instigating."

She seemed to have succeeded in hooking up the IV-pump
device. She said, "Oh, shit," looking at its underside. "I hope
we won't have to go looking for double-A batteries." Then she
seemed satisfied, because pushing a button evoked a numeral in

a little window. The next thing was to stand up and attach the other end of the tube to the bag.

But she set the whole thing aside, because a frightening contraction came over Francesca: she writhed in such an arch, her face was thrust completely under the couch. We tried to gather her, or collect her, but she just kept arching, at the most ecstatic moment rising up in a half sit-up and looking in dreamy wide-eyed astonishment at her own amazing crotch. When it was over, Thalia said, "Oh, God. Okay, I guess now, first we have to try this." And she began positioning herself like a masseuse over the body of Francesca.

"He said you have to do this hard. Or firmly. Palpate the whole thing."

She laid on hands and began, obviously, feeling for the shape of the baby in there.

"You can actually roll it," she said. "If it's facing the wrong way inside there. If it's butt-down. Like maybe her uterus *is,* possibly, able to do this but the baby is in breech presentation. That would be the idea. Like, wrong-way-in." I could tell she wasn't doing it hard enough to discern anything. The taut globe was a beach ball.

So I started setting a precedent: I took over the initiative and began this intimacy; I put my hands on the girl, and Thalia sat back when I did.

She told me as I started, "You have to feel for the head and the knees in there, and the butt. If the baby is stuck in the wrong direction, you can squash-and-squish directly *on* her and actually make the baby do a somersault so it'll be head-down. That's what you actually do," she concluded, adding one little whimper that was like a hysterical giggle just to share chagrin. That was definitely somebody, inside there. The suppleness was human, articulated for agility and getting ready to spring, already specially designated for ambition, and for all the usual unhappinesses, indeed already endowed with a rudimentary *political estate,* according to some people's philosophy. It's usually an impolite philosophy. In such impolite philosophers' defense, though, I have to admit one thing, something from old moral theology doctrine which I've found fits with life experience: a "personality" is a bodily organ, not a free-floating dialogue balloon. I couldn't say at what point, in my own history, my personality took shape inside my own mother's belly, or at what point, inside there, I took on extrinsicality and rights. I'm not exactly sure I've taken shape yet; nor been quite born yet; nor am assured, yet, of any extrinsicality or rights.

I'm not a systematic theologian; I'm a mystic. That's why I got out of the showbiz side of it, in my pulpit merely a fakir and stargazer they were tolerating, with no public rationale. For me, massaging an unborn, unrevealed potential person, through a woman's epidermal layers, is a metaphysical dream about as exalted and sublime as, say, eating a buttered potato alone at my office desk. The astonishments are all pretty much equal and equally beyond comprehension, and in fact I do rejoice over my potato. Here I was, now, finding *this* doable. I kept pushing in various places, and I was starting to show a little of the sangfroid of a surgeon. I told Thalia, "This could be its head. But it's pointy. I would rather believe this is its bottom. These could be knee or elbow areas." There was a distinct knob, probably a knee. And if I was right, the baby was already in the recommended position, head-down.

"Let me see," Thalia came forward, and tried groping. "I told Dr. Auctor about the 'incompetent uterus' issue. He said, yes, fine, but do this anyway. And John, it's a boy, by the way, they did the scan where you can see the genitals, so we don't have to call it 'it.'"

She was pressing to feel the shape inside, while her eyes gazed up through the big windows, at the blue sky, the day outdoors, which was still sunny and beautiful. We made a good team. Here she had just referred to "genitals" without the slightest self-consciousness.

She stood up, gathering together her IV equipment. "You finish this, would you?" she poured on me the mess of tubing. "It's all obvious, how it all goes, that's what he says. I'll get the needle ready. Then after that, I have to call him again and get further instructions." On a coffee table, she'd spilled out instruments from the far room. And now she got down on her knees there.

The little device had clearly marked "in" and "out" ports, but at the bottom seam of the IV bag, there were *two* plug-in places. "Which one of these do I use?"

"The one that fits the poky end of the tube. If you look? One is bigger. The end of the tube that has the little chamber. The little calibrated chamber, and the poky thing for stabbing in. Use that one."

I did as she said, and it was clear; there was only one way it might all fit together.

"The other hole," she said, "is for putting in the drugs. Putting in the anesthetic."

Also there was a little pinching clamp that must be there to prevent the "saline solution," as it was labeled, from draining out through the tube onto the floor.

"Anyway, Thalia?" I said. "I think in *my* judgment the baby is already head-down. I didn't feel a head here. It must be stuck down in." My point was, if there were no more progress, we would have to face the facts. And blame it on the patient's sealed-up uterus. And give up hoping she might give birth vaginally. If there were ever hope.

"Vertex. I think that's what it's called: vertex position," she said, and she marveled, "Somehow I know things like this."

She handed me the thick needle for the IV in its plastic cartridge. "Would you do it? Find a vein? Really. I'm going to call again. Dr. Auctor said you'll know right away when you've hit a vessel, because the little capsule fills. He said there are two things to remember: tie off the arm; and then when you stick it in, go parallel alongside the vein, not perpendicular."

Francesca was going into another contraction—her breath had quickened and she was waking from her stupor, looking around in panic.

"We've got to get some better drugs into her," Thalia said.

This contraction wasn't one of the bad ones. We both held her, but it passed without a big crisis. We just waited.

While we waited, the usual woodland sounds came from the open door. Chirp and twee of bird. Leaf shadows from sifting branches made moths on the hardwood floor. Those were west-looking windows, and I could see, as the day went deeper into afternoon the floorboards would start to shine.

"We're really a bunch of cows aren't we," Thalia said while both of us knelt over this girl.

It was a joke that alluded forward to the future, to our marriage and her fecundity and, I supposed, all women's strange risk. Last night in our hotel room we hadn't used any birth control at all, nor even mentioned the issue. That is a momentous inadvertency. I could see that's how serious we were, I approaching fifty, she almost thirty. Saying nothing about it. Imagine that. Just going ahead, at our age.

"All right," she sat back. "If you don't put the needle in, I will." It was an empty threat, purely rhetorical. So I knew I had to do it. She went over for the phone and started dialing. I picked up the needle, in its sterile cylinder. It was so big; these things are more properly called catheters instead of needles. I think that might be what they're actually called.

When she had dialed the long number for Switzerland, she plopped down on the big divan waiting for a connection, and she told me, "Once you get the needle in, you just connect the tube."

I uncapped the cartridge and inspected it. The spike was as big as the tine of a fork. I seemed to remember that, whenever I was poked with such a thing, a little bit of local, topical painkiller or something was swabbed on the skin. But our patient Francesca was already so delirious with pain, a prick from this wouldn't mean much. I lifted her pudgy forearm, where I saw nothing that

looked like a vein; the inside of the wrist looked like a likelier
spot, so I started slapping the skin, as I'd seen a nurse doing
somewhere, maybe on television—and I lowered the arm to let
gravity help fill the blood vessels. Meanwhile I looked around for
a tourniquet. The easiest thing would be the cord for the window-
blinds. It lay in loops on the floor.

Speaking into the phone, Thalia said, "Hi, it's us. Everything
worked. John's putting the needle in the arm. The baby seems to
be in position. We can't feel an obvious head anywhere. You did?
Oh well. Of course, they've got their own power failure." She
looked up at me while speaking into the phone, "I guess we go
forward, then."

She listened for a while and then said, "John?" though plainly
the doctor still had her ear, then she transmitted his advice to
me: "Turn her on her left side. Keep her on her left side. That
might increase blood flow to the uterus. It might slow down the
contractions."

I began to go about scooping her heavily to her side, away
from the couch. It wasn't hard. The patient in her unconsciousness seemed to cooperate.

Thalia, clamping the cordless between shoulder and
temple, came over and started pressing buttons on the IV
pump. "Okay, I'm holding it down. It's making the noise.
Which one is the priming button? Oh. We didn't do that.
Okay, will do." She went back to the coffee table, and her
pencil was working.

Having rolled Francesca over, I went ahead and tied off
her upper arm with the window cord, and I took a shot at
poking the needle in, with real force, a true jab, in order
not to waste time with shy half efforts. I'd chosen a spot
that showed a clear vein of blue under the skin. And as the
needle went in, I had a slightly irrelevant realization about
the human anatomy, that we're all translucent. At least above
the muscle-and-organ level. If I can see a little creek of blue,
when it's sunken a good few millimeters under the surface,

then that skin is remarkably passable by light. I was lucky and hit the vein on the first try, and a bead of color appeared inside the plastic barrel and swelled. Though I wouldn't say the "capsule filled." Thalia saw it, and she told the doctor over the phone. His response was affirmative because she nodded and raised her eyebrow for me.

Then she said, "Lignocaine?" and she turned to her pad to write again. "Lots of zeroes. I always thought adrenaline did something else. And it's two hundred at 5 percent. There's an up button and a down button. By the way, is it okay if the water bag says '5 percent Dextrose'?"

Another contraction wouldn't come for a minute. For me, there was nothing to do but wait, so I stood up, to stretch my legs.

"John? Would you find some Scotch tape or anything? And tape that needle down? Down against the skin? It shouldn't be sticking up like that." Then she went back to the telephone. "Can you just spell it? And if not, then the little white pills."

I knew exactly where a roll of tape might be in a house so orderly as this: by the phone in the kitchen, where there was a little ledge.

And sitting on it just as I'd imagined was a Scotch dispenser with green-plaid cardboard backing. I came back, and while I taped the needle down, Thalia finished her phone call and she got up and left with her flashlight, for the far room where the drug refrigerator was.

I followed her in there. She said, while she read labels on little refrigerated bottles, "Prob'ly shouldn't leave her alone. She could knock out her needle now. Did you notice all the weird animals in that room?"

I didn't answer right away, then I confirmed I had, yes, noticed.

She said, "Here it is," with a little bottle in hand. She stood up and I followed her out. "According to Bim, two hundred milliliters should be two hours' worth of unconsciousness; so this will last two hours, but he said we should be in and out of her within an hour."

So it would be a Caesarean.

As we left that trophy room, she did say—and I supposed it was a joke—"Practicing on pets, I guess."

WITH A FINGER she was rolling little pills in her open palm. "This is nitroglycerine. You give this for heart attacks. Bim says the real drug for stopping contractions isn't in the house. Nitroglycerine, he says, might kind of work in an emergency. Can't give her much, because of the baby."

When she pinched open the patient's lips and slipped the white speck into her mouth, the patient seemed to waken and take a little interest in the taste, then she laid her head down again.

Thalia stood up. She put her hands on her hips and contemplated the girl. "If it seems to work, we might give her a few grains again later. Supposedly it won't last long."

"The other drug goes in here," I suggested. I was holding the electronic device on the IV. Beneath the manufacturer's logo were the words INFUSION SYSTEM, so this was something that released small amounts of a drug into the bloodstream.

Thalia swung back on the coffee table, "Something-caine. I've got them mixed up in my mind. The main thing with that is keeping her hydrated. Meanwhile, why don't you check on the clients. Just have a look. They won't go far, but."

When I got out there, they were right outside. I'd been wrong. I'd underestimated them. They were not experimenting erotically. They were all trying to address the crisis of Francesca's trouble, in some practical manner.

And each in his own special way. The general tendency in the group is to inertia, but a couple of the leaders had prodded the others to help. Or at least behave as if they were helping. Susan the mutual fund investor had recruited Veevee to help her furnish a little soft floor of leaves and boughs that would be a cradle for the babe when it arrived. Veevee, while she did go through the motions, thought it was a terrible idea and began to complain in *my* general direction, as soon as I came out, opining loudly that people never bring newborn babies out-of-doors, and that twigs and grass would get the baby dirty even if Susan *did*, as she'd promised, find a blanket to line the nest with; but nevertheless she was kicking around listlessly in search of nest materials. The men were elsewhere. Tim was sitting at a distance on the lowest step of the house's entrance, aloof from all this, tying his shoelaces. The three others were inside the garden shed doing nothing, apparently, just standing around. When I asked them what they were up to, George confessed they were preparing the shed as a home for the mother and the baby—and of course for Tony, too—it would be a household even if only a pretend household. But this was an account he seemed to be making up on the spot, for in fact I think the three of them had been just idly exploring the tools.

"Can I have this?" said Oscar. He was holding a vicious-looking claw-like instrument.

"No, I'd better take that, and we should get out of here."

"Tony was inappropriate," Oscar recalled the scandal with pleasure.

The pleasure was contagious, and George stood on tiptoe and repeated, "He was inappropriate."

I was spreading my arms to herd them out. "Yes, he was."

George warned, just as gleefully, staying high on his tiptoes, that he was going to be hungry.

Thalia's voice came from the patio: "John, okay, we're ready. We have to start."

"Tim?" I said. He still sat at a distance. I was calling on him because he was the intelligent one here. He looked up from his seat on the lowest stair, where he had seemed to be combining his shoelace-tips in some delicate symmetrical little pattern. "Could you stay with these gentlemen here? And keep them out of trouble?"

He said, "Yeah, you'd like a rake handle up in there, wouldn't you." His smile softened to a tender snarl evaluating exactly how much I'd like a rake handle. "You'd like that, eh." He stopped smiling, then, and he got serious, reminded inwardly of some worrisome complication. He bowed over his shoelace project again.

It wasn't my place, or my job, to set him straight. Thalia, I realized, dealt with little insults and obscenities like this every day, and probably worse. But as a female she would have the moral altitude to quell insults, which as a male I don't, not in the same way. So I pretended, like a good fellow, that I hadn't heard Tim say anything.

I left them all at their projects and went inside and told Thalia that her clients were up to no mischief. They were fine. It's a little rattling, being addressed threateningly by a thirty-year-old man who seems to have no restraint of conscience. Tim is sandy haired, thin, clever looking. But his eyes have a disconsolate skittishness. They keep bouncing away. Of course, when a person grows up as peculiar, or as mentally incompetent, he's at risk of having been the victim of *actual* sodomy; I suppose at least it's a possibility in Tim's case. How else would an innocent learn about it? Moreover, how else would one learn about the social convention that values cruelty as advantageous or in any way delicious? He was, at the same time, ashamed of his aggression. Just now, in the way he was arranging his shoelace tips, he was showing a kind of fastidiousness I associate with obsessive-compulsive disorders. Such compulsions always seem to me like a form of hiding. Weaving a bower.

On the floor of the den, the patient had lifted her head again to stare wide-eyed at her own crotch, then she dropped her head back and began making a moan that was going to lift higher. There was nothing to do but wait for these things to subside. Holding her would have done nothing, as comfort, because her whole body was hardened to the point of insensitivity. Thalia, the doctor on the scene, sat beside her staring out into the daylight as if she, too, were insensible now, looking so weary.

She, my Thalia, had once been "not herself." She had lost her identity once and had now been granted a second incarnation on this earth, with no memory of her first. Who was she before? Was she "a different person" before her flight to Boise? She had had two existences, but clearly, it profits mortals not at all to increase their life on earth. Even if we are given two lives, double the mortal portion, we can stay just as unready and unwise and anxious. It's something the Hindus portray nicely, in our being reincarnated in ignorance ceaselessly. Blessed are the "poor in spirit"—that is, all the Georges and the Tonys, the Oscars and the Veevees, and this Francesca in particular lying here with no understanding of her pain, none at all. In this her only incarnation, Francesca's body was going to be forced, in a few minutes, to do something impossible. Something perhaps fatal to herself. While the rest of us smarter people might fuss uselessly. And then be waiting around just as uselessly, with the corpse, when the authorities arrive. Soon maybe the drugs would take effect. The infuser device's display window showed an illuminated number. It was attached to the drip, and the open end of its Y-connection drank like a straw from the capsule of whatever knock-out drug had come to hand.

"How long has she been getting the intravenous drug?"

Thalia didn't hear. She was looking out the window at the lawn, where the sunlight made the grass tinsel. In her station as doctor, not only was she waiting for the drug to start working, she was taking the opportunity of a lull to let her tired imagination go flat for a minute.

I knelt by the girl—her large, good face. There was nothing I could do that might help her, and I petted her bangs back from her forehead and spoke—the first word I had ever addressed to her—"Sweetheart." It was all I could say. She looked up at me with disappointment. Maybe just incomprehension. Betrayal was everywhere for this girl in her world. Who was this person, calling her sweetheart? I just sat back and tucked the loops of IV tubing away. Back when I wore my vestments and stood on the chancel, back in my absolve-bless-and-consecrate role, I used to be grateful for the parts of the old liturgy that always inserted the little apposition *I, a sinner* whenever I referred to myself. There are a number of passages where that expression appears. Those people in their teak pews, all those Sausalito neighborhood people from that hillside, they all knew me—especially the ones in the front pews—they knew how preposterous I basically am. It wasn't only my occasional mean-spirited remark or the fatuous or gossipy things they might have heard me say at one time or another, in the supermarket, or in their country clubs, or the sight of me drinking too much at a barbeque. It was also that every one of them could see me with their third eye, their omniscient eye—as this girl on the floor saw me—and all look upon me for instance in my night sweats of egoistic despair and ambition, or see me quitting the parish with a righteousness of self-disgust, insulting to all, see me despising the weak and flattering the powerful as I diligently do, see me hating Brandi McCannon, touring through pornography at my desk while drinking my five-dollar wine; we're all pretty obvious to each other. We can all picture each other. In church I might wear the leaden gown and say the mumbo jumbo (religion is such transparent poppycock and flimflam, its single justification the fact that all things, all, are transparent poppycock and flimflam), but amid the mumbo jumbo, also, I would get to say publicly in that church, for my own ears, "I, a sinner," and that might be the only historical part, the one part with some meaning.

Thalia answered my long-lost question, as it still hung out there, "I just now got it going." She meant the general-anesthetic drip. She was still staring out the window.

In fact, even as I watched Francesca's face, the expression of fixed grief was fading, falling into a more dreamy confusion. It was working. She was obtaining a little mercy.

SO SHE WAS making a successful journey to Gilead, where there is a balm. But it meant my own trial was about to begin.

Nevertheless, half the time, I continued to have a sneaky abiding, dreamy feeling I could somehow be out of the room when it was time for cutting. I would find some excuse. I didn't have any distinct *plan* of cowardice, but just a fairy-tale feeling, an inward promise—partly just a conviction of how *bad an idea* it was, for the girl's blood to spread on the hardwood floor under my hand. I didn't *specifically* picture myself outside on the lawns with the clients. Or in the bathroom. Or distancing myself by hiking up the driveway, toward the exit gate between the rows of Auctor's tall eucalyptus trees. Yet some evasion might still come along. Maybe a cab or an ambulance would arrive early, in time. It's only by *not* thinking that one goes forward. Instruments of chrome steel lay on the mosaic-topped coffee table where Thalia had poured them clanking down, and having rested her mind long enough, she went over and collected them, raking them together in handfuls for transport to the kitchen to be boiled. She had already started a big pot of water on the stove.

An alarming rattle, just then, drummed on the coffee table. It was my cell phone vibrating. The music of "Night on Bald Mountain" swirled up.

I told her it would just be Brandi.

Which meant I wouldn't answer.

She looked down at the display window of the phone. "It's Coldwell Banker. It's probably your friend Ted. You don't want to know?"

No. This was not the time. I let it go on ringing.

"You don't care about Brandi's sales volume?"

Not just then, I didn't care. That morning when we were still at the Silverado Resort, I had called my own office. The Sunday anchor agent was my friend Ted Cleland, and he called somebody he knew at the Century 21 castle and asked them to go through the faxes, where indeed there was a new offer from Brandi McCannon. The new asking price was sixteen thousand dollars less than before. I had an idea that this would be the amount Shawn and Cheese had misplaced, in their market speculations. Brandi, in the new offer, was taking dual agency, representing both buyer and seller, which was what I'd expected. But the strange thing was, she was only taking 3 percent, not charging Edna for the other 3 percent she could have taken. Ted, who knew something of the inner workings at Century 21, had a possible explanation, involving Brandi's total annual sales-volume rewards at her office. There might be some goal she aimed to exceed, and so qualify for a better broker-agent split for the entire year's volume. He said he would call me back. (This phone conversation took place when the day was still uncomplicated, while I sat at a café table overlooking the Silverado golf course, with coffee and juice.) I asked him meanwhile to fax Brandi's office, warning her on Coldwell Banker letterhead that I was going to go to the Board of Realtors to have her censured.

Thalia went on collecting all her shiny sharp tools together, and we both let the music of the telephone play on. The ringtone is joined into a loop. So it keeps swinging back up to the most maddened, stormiest part, where the most terrible powers of darkness are summoned in a whorl over that Bald Mountain. At last it stopped, leaving us to our own rites here, isolated as we were. Thalia was carrying the whole bouquet of chrome steel blades and clamps into the kitchen, plus the cordless phone. "I'm calling again. Would you come and boil these?"

On the stove, the water was already steaming. Thalia had poured the whole slew of tools out on the countertop, and I looked around for some kind of kitchen gadget—tongs or something—because if I was going to drop all these instruments in the water I would need a way of plucking them out later.

"Hi," she said into the phone, as she went into the far chamber of medical equipment, flashlight in hand. "It worked. She's gone under. I couldn't find any antibiotic. But I'm going back in there right now. All right. I'll tell him heart rate."

I started dropping the surgical tools in the water separately— broad scissors and skinny scissors, curved scissors and extremely short-beaked scissors, tweezers, tweezers that had a lock for holding their grip. No knives, curiously. Then more scissoring tools, but hinged like tongs: backward-hinged tongs that didn't grip things together, but rather forced things apart—and then locked with ratcheted teeth to hold them apart.

Thalia came out with other tools—among them some little blades—and she dropped her new handful in the water, then carried bottles and sponges and plastic sheeting out to the living room. "John?" she said, "Help me look for something. It's very important to have a cautery—a thing called a cautery—and I can't find one."

I followed her back into the dark medical storage room while she described it: a cautery was a little battery-powered thing that was supposed to look like a Magic Marker, with a tip that gets hot. "You touch it to bleeding tissue," she said. "It burns the little capillaries and stops bleeding. He says it's absolutely indispensable. If we don't have it, there'll be too much blood everywhere."

I undertook to start looking systematically through the dozens of shallow drawers. She kept searching the many cupboards. She was the one with the flashlight, so my own search was slow and painstaking working in the indirect flicker. Meanwhile we were losing precious time during the patient's period of sleep, and at last I said—it had crossed my mind right away, but seemed ridiculous—"I noticed a soldering gun."

I went back to the kitchen. It was in the drawer where the flashlight had been. Shaped like a pistol, but with a single thick spike on the tip to get hot and melt electrical circuits together, it ought to serve the purpose of cauterizing. I'd actually never handled a soldering gun, but I'd seen them used.

Thalia had followed me out into the kitchen, and she looked at it and said, "Well . . . that should work."

But then I noticed the pronged electrical plug at the end of its cord. I held the plug up for her.

"Oh, well," she said. "I'll call back again and ask if there's some other way, because we *really* don't want the patient to lose blood. He says it's also a problem for *us*. If blood's on the floor, it's slippery, and we slip and it's a mess. I'll go back. Meanwhile, would you get that stuff out of the water? We're going to have to start. He's going to talk us through this. With or without the cautery, we have to do this."

I DIDN'T BOTHER with tongs, I simply poured the whole pot out in the sink, to let the chromy blades clatter out and the water drain.

I was in a hurry because I had another idea. Beside the stove was a set of kitchen knives. I turned on the stove burner and left the blue gas flame flaring high, and I tried propping one of the knives on its handle so its blade would extend into the flame. A wooden cutting board, which I pulled into place, was the right height to rest a knife handle on, and I lined up several knives, their blades thrust into two different rings of flame. These could do the cauterizing, if they got hot enough to make cut flesh sizzle.

Thalia came bursting past. "Can you take her blood pressure again? And get the heart rate beats per minute? I'm going to do the 'prep.' As it's called. By people who know what they're doing."

She stopped and came back and watched what I was accomplishing, but watched rather skeptically. "Maybe that's a good idea."

"It seems like the metal might get hot enough," I said. "We would have to keep an eye on them. Somebody'll have to monitor them. And make sure they don't . . ."

Whatever. Catch fire. I lifted one out to see if it had begun to glow red. It hadn't.

"Well, maybe it's a good idea," she said, again, as she crossed over and picked scalpels and clamps out of the sink basin, collecting them in a hand to take them to the living room. "Maybe one of the kids could keep an eye on the stove, then. Letting the patient lose blood is the worst thing, he says."

I got a total of five carving knives lined up, roasting over two stove burners, then I stood back, and before turning my back, with my palms I packed a spell around the whole construction, keeping it from falling apart. Thalia had left a few sterilized instruments in the sink, which I collected. Out in the living room, she was kneeling. With the phone on her shoulder, she dragged the afghan coverlet down off the ball-shaped belly of Francesca, then she hunched down closer, and at a certain tropic slope below the girl's great bulge she swabbed a solution from a plastic bottle directly onto Francesca's skin. "Right here," she said.

The unattractive frizzy vaginal opening, squashed into a little frown by the mound of life above it, bid for my dull attention in a ricochet of the eye, but I had been asked to take blood pressure, and the blood pressure cuff was nowhere to be seen. Where had I put it? I first went to the coffee table to lay out the rest of the sterilized instruments in good order—scissors here, blades there, from smallest to largest—and Thalia got up and stood over them, considering them all. She complained on the phone to Dr. Auctor, "They all look alike. The towel clamp is gonna look like all the forceps and whatever." She added, grimly, "I found the retractors."

She turned to me. "Wash your hands, John. Forget the blood pressure."

I went off to the kitchen to do as she said, with a squirt of dish soap at the sink and by passing my shining hands back and forth over each other in the ancient and archetypal gesture of detachment and even blamelessness. In twenty-four hours Thalia and I together were passing through milestone stages on life's way, a marriage and now a birth and, possibly yet, a death. Many are the hospital beds I've stood beside, and in some sense presided over—but presiding over the invisible passages only—leaving the practical matters to the nurses as they mop up, tuck away, fold back, their stoicism and their polite reserve implying the superfluity of the priest's little objects, the ewer and goblet, the plate, the linen napkin.

I could hear Thalia in the living room telling Dr. Auctor, "She's pink. I'd say she's superpink. But honestly, I don't know how pink she usually is," and I loved Thalia at that moment rather irrelevantly, she was so brave. When I came back with holy hands upraised (as I'd seen on TV), she was administering injections to the area above the girl's pubis. She had put the cordless on the floor, where it lay listening, and her needle stung the girl's flesh in several places along a horizontal line. When she was done, she sat back on her ankles, and I could see she'd used a pen—there was the black Sharpie marker on the floor—to mark a long dash on the belly above the pubic hair. It was the guide. Along it she had injected the anesthetic, raising five mosquito bites at intervals on its length.

She lodged the phone on her shoulder again and told Dr. Auctor, "The lignocaine's in."

She had a second syringe in hand and, with a wince and a show of clumsy frailty, snapped off its cap. "How will I know if I'm hitting past the abdominal wall?"

Then she looked to me and said, "John, we're going to wait a minute for the drug to work, and then cut. We have to get in and out fast, because she's going to lose blood, and lose blood pressure. So we want to be efficient."

I knelt at the mound. This was an interesting question in personality construction: how I was getting through this. For one thing, my posture now, kneeling, was an avid Boy-Scout-at-a-campfire attitude, which made this seem more fun than scary. I'd knelt at projects before. In such ways, so far, this was something I could do.

"Basically he says it's skin, then muscle walls, then some membranes, and pulling out the baby. You keep sponging blood.

You clamp off a blood vessel if it's . . . if blood is coming out. You try to cauterize all the bleeding tissue. And I'll be sponging and sponging." She had in fact collected a few sponges and a mountain of towels behind her on the floor. "The main job is afterward: sewing back the different layers. After the baby is free. That is what's risky and complicated, and it's what's time-consuming. Going in goes fast."

She lifted the phone and spoke into it, "All right," then listened to the voice in Zurich. She said, "I'll call you again in a few minutes," and she put the phone to rest, over on the coffee table.

She got up. Scanning her new list, she was going to disappear into the far room again. "He says he tried calling Marin General to learn about her case. But he couldn't get through. I've got to find some things. You prepare a bowl of warm salt water, it can just be tap water, warm, and lots and lots more towels. Bath towels, sheets, moppy things. Also, dear heart"—she stopped and turned and looked at me, tilting her head in that way that made her hairstyle's one parenthesis poke her jaw—in that expression *dear heart* was a full pulse of affection, and gratitude for everything I was doing right now—"would you go get the clients? Recruit anybody with the ability for it? Some of them might mop. Some of them might hold retractors."

WHEN YOU START cutting, at least in the case of a pregnancy, the belly skin is stretched so elastic, at the first sketching of a blade it parts like a smile broadly. I followed the five-inch line Thalia had drawn with a Sharpie, and under the blade the gap opened in a curious *silence*. The soundlessness of the cut was dreamy, and buttery, and I was beginning to think I would be able to do this whole thing without revulsion or any kind of instability. Thalia, holding a big carving knife whose blade had been in the fire, was standing in the kitchen doorway, where she could keep an eye on the rest of the knives as they heated. She had the phone at her ear, and she told me, "You should be getting into a layer of fat. He says keep stroking down through it. Just stop when you hit the fascia. The fascia will be white."

She told the doctor in Zurich, "I guess we did the anesthetic right."

That kitchen knife idea, as we went on, seemed to be working out. She gave it a try holding the hot blade against a section of open tissue, which wasn't bleeding fast, just sweating fine red drops—and with a little kiss sound it had the effect not of blackening it but stealing all color, turning it beige. Oddly, there wasn't much bleeding as I went along. The gash grew as two dry lips with only pinpoint droplets expanding; and beneath that, golden curds of fat, but no blood to speak of. No fast gushes or even steady leaks. Thalia mentioned this to the doctor on the phone, but I didn't hear anything of what the answer was. Apparently it didn't indicate a problem. Then there was one area of seeping and filling, so Thalia quickly went back in and got a freshly heated knife from the stove, and she tiptoed forward and applied it. It smoked and made its hiss, and it seemed to work. After I'd sponged out the filled area, it started filling again, but much slower, and then it never welled over. The barbeque smell was something I wasn't going to be bothered by.

In her Raggedy Ann smock, Susan stood by holding up a sponge. She was unfazed by the gore. Also Veevee had shown up to help; she looked more disgusted and worried than Susan, but Veevee always, rain or shine, wears an expression as if there were a bitter taste in her mouth—it's so permanently fixed that vertical creases are etched around her lips, whether she's witnessing an abdominal operation or riding in a car watching the Sonoma countryside go by. Among the clients, only the females had the courage to assist. The four men were useless. Embarrassed or afraid, they all preferred to stay outside and stand together in a clump on the patio, in their vests of fluorescent orange. They never conversed much, but they gravitated together.

With so little blood, the hot knife blade wasn't needed, and Thalia mostly just watched. Susan held up her square blue sponge— not a surgical sponge, it was one of those kitchen Scotch-Brites with an absorbent side and a textured side for scouring nonstick pans, which I'd popped out of its three-pack cellophane. There were other, more official-looking sponges, but that was the one Susan picked. (This was not going to be a perfectly sterile operation. Thalia had been warned by Dr. Auctor that the most important job, once we got Francesca to a real hospital, would be to fight infections. We'd failed to turn up any antibiotics.) I myself was performing rather well, cutting competently, until I got down to the fascia. At that point—going through the fascia—it was the *sound* of dissection that made me know how actual was the situation, of entering into

another human being. I was using a pair of specialized scissors—
one blade spatulate and blunt, for sliding underneath a surface,
the other blade normal—and the convening blades in cutting the
human fabric made a crisp sound, and then once I'd cut through the
fascia, inside the slippery slimy tough bag (referred to as the perito-
neum), the thick uterus itself, between closing scissor blades, made a
crunchy vinyl noise under the snip, because evidently a uterine wall
is a resilient, supple material. The fine-grained snip sound was what
made me turn away, a yeast multiplying fast in my mouth, and I got
up off my knees and went outside. I was blacking out. I wanted to
get away from that smell, the live mud smell, and the sensation that
my own human heart had been placed in my mouth, exactly filling
my oral cavity. In the role of surgeon, if I were to faint or vomit right
there, I would be merely adding to the day's troubles. Outside in the
fresh air and afternoon light and all the usual lawn sounds, it was
like coming up from underwater.

I couldn't speak, but I'd waved as I left, indicating I wasn't
deserting them, I would be back. Maybe I just had to throw up.
Maybe in the hedgerow. The developmentally disabled men outside took no notice of me. I sat down on the floor out there—the
smooth flagstones of Dr. Auctor's patio—and I folded my ankles
together and hung my head and observed the pattern of stitching
on my socks. Chirps and warbles. The *chuck-chuck* of a squirrel.
Dappled shade. The sun of Sonoma County in its kaleidoscope
was fattening and sweetening wine grapes all over the mountain-
sides. I wondered how much of an hour had elapsed. When a taxi
might appear at the outer gate. Or Sandy appear. I evidently lost
consciousness. But I didn't fall over, or even roll over gently onto
the flagstones, because when I recovered my awareness, I was
still hanging over my crossed ankles. The difference was, with
the passage of time, Tim had gone in. It was only three of them
standing outside, George and Oscar and Tony.

I looked through the window and saw Tim's head bowed
where mine had been, over the origin of the world. He had taken
over as surgeon, so it seemed.

I felt strong enough, so I stood up and I came inside—not just strong enough but insulted enough, or guilty enough, while also a little glad for this turn of events and, surprisingly, amazingly *confident* that Tim, of all people, could have the right competence for this. With his IQ of seventy-five. Thalia looked up at me with a resigned shrug. "He was very insistent."

Still, the salty smell of blood was in the room, as well as the singed-flesh smell because Thalia had been applying the heated carving-knife blade. She said of the knife cautery, "This does work," while she got up off her knees and went to the kitchen to trade for a hotter one. I could see her at the stove where she made garden-bed adjustments in the blades as they roasted, pulling some partway out. When I came over to the rim of the operation, Tim had reached deep into the wound. One hand was wrist-deep. The other was poking in more gingerly, trying to pluck at some part of the baby through the gash that brimmed with fluid. Wearing the same deadpan expression as if he were watching television, he kept exploring with the ladle of a hand.

"The head is still down," he told Thalia. The tone was, this was a problem. The head was somehow stuck. The wound in the belly was an open dolphin's mouth around his wrist. How can surgeons do what they do? I can't imagine the bravery, or thoughtlessness. They handle these irreplaceable, sacred parts, in their slime. Back in med school they choose a specialty like obstetrics before they've even had a baby of their own! Is it just callow precociousness? At least I chose a livelihood innocuous and inconsequent putting on black cloth as I did. It's almost fiendish what doctors are able to do, having put on white.

"You gotta get its head up," Thalia told her developmentally disabled partner. "He said find the lips." (The unattached *he* always referred to the doctor in Switzerland.) "If you can find the mouth, find it. And actually stick your finger in his little mouth, and that will put his head right. It makes him flip his head back. Veevee? Do you have your turkey baster? Have that ready, sweetie. Be ready with it." I was aware of a certain peripheral sight but didn't look directly at it: Veevee had been discharging turkey baster–loads of rich red blood into a bowl.

Susan, sponge lifted and poised, spoke over her shoulder to her friend Veevee, "Don't worry, she's not dead."

Veevee snapped, "I know she isn't dead."

There must have remained only a little amniotic fluid after her water broke. A thinly diluted blood had rolled out over the floor, but it wasn't much. Thalia had packed a berm of terrycloth bath towels all around the patient's butt. My stomach now promised not to be so weak anymore, and I picked up a dry bath towel, to make myself useful.

Then with a rubbery shudder the dolphin's mouth disgorged a baby human head. It combined fairy tale and nightmare seeing the effigy of a perfect doll appear, its eyes bitterly shut, handsome looking, not plump or baby-like but skinny, showing already certain signs of character like a bust of a Roman emperor. Character traits that baby fat would soon cloud over. Not to reemerge until the age of forty or so. All this time, there'd been someone in there waiting for this to happen.

It was blue in color, and I knew that was normal, yet even knowing it's normal, the blueness is worrisome. Also, the dolphin's gargling mouth still retained the doll's shoulders. So maybe there was going to be some further wrestling and prying, or some further cutting. At this development I wouldn't be able, anymore, to come near the now two-headed creature on the floor. It was a lucky thing Tim had taken over. Emotionally disabled child-man, he was better equipped, with a blankness of imagination. I knew Thalia would forgive my cowardice. A woman gets the husband she gets, and learns to cultivate his mix of skills and deficiencies. She works around him. I used to observe this in my marriage counseling. A husband can be a huge inconvenience (he can sometimes be an inconvenience on a colossal scale), or he might be an asset, too, but a husband is really only an accessory in a mature woman's true life, which is an inner life, with its own agendas, a life so deep it will be dark even to the most attentive husband, himself little guessing how peripheral he is, though he be at the center too. Now, today, all I was able to do was admire Thalia.

Which was easy. As she approached with her ready knife, there was no fast bleeding. I wasn't worried anymore. It seemed plain that the tissues could be stitched together fast enough that the mother would be all right. And the baby was handsome. The baby looked like Tony. He had thick black hair and a hairline like Tony's. It was *somebody*, lifting up its head, with its infant's palsied tremor; it had long since fashioned itself into somebody according to its own inner algorithms. I wondered if Tony and Francesca had decided on a name. He would soon get fat and fill out the usual mold, but at his birth his face showed as much character as Abe Lincoln.

My cell phone on the table began singing its stormy song, and to shut it up, hating it, I snatched it up and answered it, even though it was Brandi. She was the last person I wanted to dicker with right now, but the strange thing was, I simply wanted to tell her the good news, it stood blazing on my crown, and I flipped open the phone and cried, "Brandi!"

"Ah, John, we've got a problem."

"You'll never guess what's just happening. I'm in Sonoma. I can't talk, but this is the most amazing thing right here. Do you have power?"

"No, everything's out everywhere. But we've got cell. Thank God for cell. What did we do before cell? Anyway, John, my clients Shawn and Cheese are unhappy. They're unhappy with being told they have to be married. They're talking about taking legal action and—ha!—revoking your license. I have tried to tell them. They have no sense. We all know it was only a joke, and *they* know it was only a joke, but they think they've got a technicality, and that's how they're talking."

"Oh? Did I violate their civil rights?"

This was her retaliation for my threat of going to the Board of Realtors. It would come to nothing. In fact, the idea was so flimsy

I couldn't see what was on Brandi's mind. She's not stupid. She must have been thinking only that she would need to be able to point to some plausible excuse for stealing Edna away from me. Something she could tell the board. The whole thing cheered me up, for some reason: it only meant that the world would still be revolving on its usual wheel when I got back on Monday morning, and I was glad for the prospect, given what I'd been looking at on this floor.

"I'm your friend, John, and I know what you meant, but they've looked up the Fair Housing Act, and they're going to call it discriminatory. Have you noticed there's no such thing as a joke anymore? Joking is illegal? *I* know you were joking. You were joking! I know you couldn't have *not* been joking. But there's no such thing as a joke anymore."

The whole baby was coming out. Under my very eyes, it was going to slide out, exactly like the packaged pork tenderloin that, in my own kitchen sink a few days ago, had slid from its tough Safeway shrink-wrap with its lubrication of slime. The baby was a miniature Tony, and it was flapping its little rubbery blue arms to get a swimmer's grasp on this world.

"Brandi," I said. I just wanted to get her off the phone and *not* share this miracle with her. "Those little fuckers *ought* to be married."

"Well, John, of course you're right. In *that* sense, you're absolutely *not* joking, it *isn't* funny, not in the slightest, they should be married, but you're my friend, John. I know you have moral, philosophical, ethical *things* about this. People should be married, but I can still see a way we can save this situation."

It made me love Brandi, in a way, Brandi in her constant, unsleeping nickel-and-dime scheming, never married, solitary, auburn-red of hair, aerobic in personality, rumored never to date, member of the Mensa high-IQ club, lover of steeple-racing horses on weekends, lover of crewing on sailboats in San Francisco Bay, riser at 5 AM every day to get a jump on everybody and read the papers and do her exercises at the gym; Brandi suddenly felt like my sister, and I wanted her to go ahead and *have* both ends of the sale on Edna Goodkind's bungalow if she wanted. Edna would do all right with her. Edna would get to Reward Village with Brandi McCannon, too.

"Hell with those kids," I said pushing the joke. "They're fornicators, let 'em be banished to outer darkness," I tried to distort the thing to extremes, because I know sometimes my own idea of sarcasm can be too subtle and I can be taken literally.

I didn't intend to hang up then so abruptly, but something had started happening. All the other clients had come inside, having sensed a commotion, and they were worried by what they saw. The infant had been turned away from me, so I hadn't noticed anything.

The problem was, the new baby had a slight defect! It was one of us! The little tough rubbery thing as it was lifted free (its twisty live belly cord still attached) turned to face the light, and an entire lobster was clinging to, or embedded in, the side of its head, engulfing its ear and jaw and temple. It was a hemangioma. Thalia, too, would recognize it, because in Group there were two different young kids whose (not nearly so extensive) hemangiomas had been removed. Over the marred baby Thalia and I shared a glittering wince, of fretfulness, for it probably would require a course of several operations for surgeons to remove the little purple beast, and it looked like it involved the right eye, so it might be complicated.

I moved around toward helping. He would have to be washed and wrapped, I supposed. The banishment of Brandi McCannon's voice had reestablished the possibility of order. New midafternoon sun was finding a luster in the hardwood floor. I decided maybe I could show some fortitude and start helping get the wound sewn up—which after all was supposed to be the trickier part, and I tossed the phone into a chair, because I was feeling fine. After the passage of the child, the hole had shrunken to a very small mouth again. Nothing was bleeding. The next important thing was to get it closed. I could get down and do that.

"Have you discussed a name?" Thalia asked nobody in particular. She looked around and found Tony planted far away by the door. "Have you and Francesca thought about a name?"

Tony only shook his head, staying by the door. Most of the other clients had fled, stealthily, after the baby's disfigurement was revealed. Except for Susan the Raggedy Ann girl, they'd left and weren't visible anywhere on the patio. Tony had stopped in the doorway, but he was looking wary, and he told us both, "They can cut that off," summoning defiance, forming his hard frown.

She told him, "He's beautiful. You're right, though, Tony. That lump is normal, and it can be removed. He'll have a prosperous life."

In that estimate of his son, he seemed to take Thalia's word, because he frowned more deeply in approval. Still he stayed where he was in the doorway.

I'd run lurching out of the operating room at the most important moment, but now for some reason I felt fine, and I thought I could stay and work and not falter. Thalia located a pair of shiny chrome scissors and, making no ceremony of it, snipped the umbilical cord, which made the fine crunch sound again, but this time it wasn't so sickening; it was satisfying. Or at least it was the sound of a necessity. Blood didn't come from the cut cord, as I'd always supposed it would. Then the magical long, flexible, metaphysical hyphen would have to be tied up. But I could see a clamp, which at some point Thalia had clipped on it. Which explained why it hadn't bled, maybe.

"Can I trust you with this?" she asked Susan the mutual funds investor, the one who hadn't run away. The baby needed to be wrapped. One of the bath towels had come to hand, and Thalia offered the towel-plus-baby combination.

So the baby—who was conscious and showing patience with this ordeal, not complaining—was then swaddled tight in terrycloth by the hands of Thalia and Susan together, lying between them on the floor where they knelt—then he was passed across to Susan.

Oscar, of all people, was the first curious one who came back, showing up outside in the window to spy in on the scene, cupping his hands around his eyes at the glass. Then Veevee, who seemed to find his curiosity objectionable, came up behind him and pulled him back out of sight.

"We have to clean the baby up," said Thalia, with distinct happiness, for we were all doing well. "And we have to get the placenta out." With tacky red hands she picked up the cordless phone and hit redial.

The placenta-removal part—which I pictured as a kind of scraping, and which Tim would have undertaken if he were still in the room—was an operation I was, yet, willing to try. But Thalia while she dialed the phone said, "I'm going to go find Tim," and I was just as happy to let the responsibility fall elsewhere. So I followed Susan into the kitchen, where she carried the new boy to wash him off. The baby, little godlet, continued to squint mystically into the blur, stoically up past the towering faces. He hadn't even cried yet. I started the tap flowing to get the water temperature up. The only thing to do was put him directly under the tap, right in the sink. It was a big-enough sink. Susan was holding the doll to her bosom, the purple cauliflower of his cheek against the bib of her Raggedy Ann smock. To entertain him she made little fish-mouth yawns and bubbles at him.

One odd outcome I couldn't help but notice was that I, the competent one, was not especially useful. I was even pointedly excluded, the defective ones here as competent as I, Tim especially, who had shown the strength and dexterity of a surgeon. I stood there with my hand under the faucet while the water was getting to be warm, but at that point Thalia called from the other room: "Susan? Dr. Auctor says spread out the towel on the floor, and put the baby on the floor unwrapped. *While* you wash him. Let him get cold, and let him get a little exercise. Let him shiver, even. You want to get his whole blood supply everywhere."

I watched while she unfolded the papoose on the floor. How *scrawny* is a healthy newborn. Envisioning the future, in general terms, I pictured a slow painful recovery for Francesca, in which, however, she would display almost no self-pity, characteristically. She would first find her son's facial blemish worrisome. Eventually, superficial surgeries would fix that. Soon enough, she would take an interest in the infant. However, there would also be days of complete indifference, and even forgetfulness, concerning the (as she might see it) new "little brother." All the mothering would be done by the grandmother, or by the grandmothers plural. From my few observations of the Down syndrome personality, I tend to believe Francesca will see the new sibling in the sunniest light, as a fresh playmate, but a disappointing one over the years, and there might be episodes of resentment over how much attention it will divert to itself. As for the boy, born with a normal IQ, he is fated for a more difficult life than some, but also a gifted life. He'll have a mother who is his inferior, which will furnish certain learning experiences.

After Susan had pulled apart the blanket on the kitchen floor and exposed the baby to air, it was only then that the fellow gave out his first cry, starting with preliminary tremors. The sound wasn't a complaint; it was more an announcement, merely grouchy. On his cheek the hemangioma lay open to inspection. It looked now mostly shallow, but extensive, and fixing it would be costly, but he was a Marin County babe, so maybe at least one of the grandmothers could foot the bill, work to be done at the Auctor clinic of course. Best in the field. As for me, I was done with Group. I would get along all right without a harelip's protection. No doubt I would find some other personal defect to hold dear. Thalia, using a tone aimed for me, spoke from the other room: "We've got about an hour and fifteen minutes of anesthesia left. We got the placenta."

So she was offering: she wanted me to do the hard part, and take over from Tim. Who came into the kitchen to wash his hands, not making eye contact with anyone, dully.

Thalia in the den was getting to her feet with some stiffness, and she came to the kitchen passageway bringing me a pair of the scissor clamps that closed and locked. And a needle and thread.

"Here's what you do."

She had taken instructions over the phone. The needle, in her bloody fingers, was curved like a fingernail paring, with thread already attached. "You get a grip on the needle with the forceps, on this end here. And then you squeeze it to lock it. See, now you've got a good handle. So you can really *hold* the needle. 'Cause you have to force it through."

Having demonstrated, she offered it out to me: a needle clenched in a small chrome beak. "There's different kinds of stitches, but he says it doesn't matter: just do it sloppy: a real doctor, anyway, will have to redo it for us. Just stitch it however. Don't put in a lot of stitches. He says get her to a hospital as soon as somebody gets here, and keep her chock-full of Oramorph."

So I would have to do this. I took the forceps and the needle to practice getting the grip. But then, first of all, I went over to the sink, to scrub my hands again with dishwashing liquid. I knew what would happen with those two kids, Brandi's buyers. They would get their house. And have a big party. I knew I had been unwise, and I'd been somewhat less than humble. Let them pretend to be irate. Because they had a right. A house isn't a marriage, but it might be a way to start. There was a discussion I saw once in PreachIt.org about the efficacy of sacraments "among even the doubters." Something on a text of Augustine's. What caught my eye at the time was that it had to do with unworthy ministers—"as for the proud minister, he is to be ranked with the devil," and other such boilerplate. But there was something about how a sacrament can be efficacious even in defiled hands, something about "passing through a corrupted minister intact," to reach "fertile earth." So, gowned as well as I ever would be for the job of surgery, I came out with upraised hands, ready to get down on my knees before the wounded girl who slept so solidly. During the whole baby removal, her stomach muscles had been parted like curtains, held apart by one of the stretching devices from the coffee table. But now since the device had been removed, the entire gaping cavity had shrunk back to a little mouth again, and the girl herself had of course gotten smaller.

"Gotta shitload of Oramorph," Thalia remarked. A sisterly vulgarity was licensed by our success here, and by the new partnership. She was examining the label on a bottle of pills with a bleary closeness. "We should take her blood pressure. Though she's looking rosy, isn't she. Sandy ought to get here soon. Any minute. We should post one of our people out at the gate. It's been almost an hour."

"If I'm going to have room to work here, I need the retractors put back," I said, using the right technical word as I'd heard it used.

But meanwhile I was going right past the patient. I actually strolled out the open door. I hadn't planned any exit, but my body needed clear air, so I just stood on the doormat outside, holding up my clean, wet hands where the direct heat of the falling sun could attach to them. All the clients were all over the gardens. On their own initiative they had taken up rakes and pruning shears and hedge clippers and gone to work. The jobs they'd picked weren't necessarily the most important tasks—one might be merely raking pea gravel back and forth; another with pruners seemed to take little ornamental bites out of a leaf—but they were staging a drama of hard work for their own moral pleasure. It was a scene in the medieval Book of Hours, where on a series of pages, a feudal estate is illustrated in all the months of the year, farmers looking more like lords and ladies, in soft slippers and veils, under a lapis sky tilling the earth, making all labor look like a minuet, obeying the command to dress the earth and keep it. Those artists who made those pages had access to such pigments—sky blue, brass, clover green—it makes the eye thirsty, and the soul thirsty, too. I'm probably the type who might have lived in the Middle Ages, if only things, then, were so ideal as that picture.

Francesca's uterine wall was so thick and slippery the meat layers tended to squirt out even from between the tightest pinch, and I could see right away—before I was even able to get the needle in at all—a proper pair of forceps would be necessary like pliers to get a hold on the edges. The forceps worked perfectly—they weren't going to bruise the tissue—and after that, it all looked straightforward, the wound small enough now to just about let a baseball pass. The whole boy had come through that. I found I could first use the grips to force the little crescent pin through one side, and then when it emerged on the other side, use a second pair of grips to pull it through. Thalia said, "I've got these. Look. Butterfly bandages, so we won't have to use a needle at all on the incision." The first three stitches looked good. I didn't pull very tight. I only planned to put in a dozen or so, along the length of the gap, because within an hour a real surgeon would be working on her. Meanwhile, the baby in the kitchen had been rewrapped—its crying had stopped—the one here who had no name yet. That seemed remarkable: that there should be someone in this house right now who had no "name," swirling like a koan. Susan came out of the kitchen carrying the wrapped boy, and she went over and stood with him by the window, to let light fall on him.

Thalia was heading out the door to the patio, saying, "Dear heart, now, I think I'd better go out and put somebody out at the gate. I won't be gone long. I'll be back before you need anything."

She went out, and Susan followed. So I was left all alone in the house, in the room, with this naked, supine, plump young woman we'd drugged and maimed, crouched over her: it seemed an indecent situation, funnily, but I'd been trusted with it. Thalia said she wouldn't be gone long, and the whole closing-up operation might take ten minutes at the most. The stitches were going in well enough. Knowing it didn't matter how perfect this was, because my rough work would be redeemed by a real surgeon, I poked and pulled with confidence, kneeling in the gore. With an amusing thought actually. I certainly didn't laugh, but I did get a little pang of absurdity to think if somebody happened to come in right now and found me like this alone with the girl in the whole scene, they would think I was up to something so dastardly, so perverted, so much from the sickest unenterable extremes of, like, baadboy.com or someplace it would be unimaginable.